1

Also, by Patrick Langridge

Bound for carnage

BOUND
FOR
RETRIBUTION

1

The last two years have gone by in a blur. Stan's place
has all been rebuilt. I have my own little pad in the
grounds too. Danny is getting around like a whippet on
his new prosthetic leg. We've been busy helping a few
people out with some problems. The weapons have
remained in Stan's armoury, that's always a good thing,
and Sally has moved out here with the girls. It was
around a year after John was killed that they moved out
here. Sally had drifted away from friends and the girls
weren't happy at school, so she asked me to help her
start a new life in L.A. She also told me that since John's
death, she had received a few threatening letters from
some old clients of his. They moved into my place until
they sorted themselves out. I was happy to have a room
at Stan's for a while. Recently they moved to their own
apartment downtown. Plus, Stan and Carol now have a
thing going. Didn't see that coming. She was all ready to
move on and start life again, but when Stan took her out

for a meal before she left, they hit it off. To cut a long story short, she didn't leave.

It was about six months ago where this next story started.

Sally and the girls had been out here for around five months. They were settled and happy. We were all pretty much content with life, at that point. Sally had made some new girlfriends. The girls were settled in a new high school. I was actually pretty happy with the way things were going. There was one night, where the girls were out on a sleepover and Sally and I were just relaxing watching a movie. The wine tasted great and the conversation was flowing. By the end of the evening, we ended up sleeping together. The following day was slightly awkward, but we eventually agreed to never talk about it and move on.

The girls were getting quite close to me by now, calling me uncle Mike, which I kind of liked. I felt responsible for their well-being, Sally's too. We took the girls for a long weekend in Santa Barbara, nice town, great food, and lovely beaches. We had a lot of fun and it was good to see the three of them smiling. The hotel was lovely. I had a separate room, obviously. It was a shame that we had to go back home after such a great weekend. The girls had school. Sally had work. I also had things to do, but we did agree to do it again soon.

2

It was a Saturday morning, around nine, nine thirty. As I was down as Sally's emergency contact at the beauty salon where she worked, they called me.

"Hello." I said.

"Hi, is that Mike?"

"It is. Who's this?"

"Hi sorry, this is Dana, Sally's boss."

"Hi, how can I help."

"I was just wandering if Sally was, ok? She hasn't turned in for work this morning, and I thought maybe she'd just forgotten to call."

"Right, that is strange. She dropped her girls off to me this morning and left for work."

"I know she doesn't usually work weekends. I can reschedule her clients for her, just wanted to check she is ok."

"I will try and get hold of her."

"Thank you. Just ask her to let me know if she will be in as usual on Monday morning."

"Will do."

I ended the call, and called Sally straight away. No answer. I tried a few times and was greeted with an answerphone every time. I called Stan and asked if the girls could hang out there for a bit. I needed to go and check on Sally. As usual he was as helpful as ever, and Danny had offered to keep an eye on them.

Once the girls were settled, I got in my car and drove downtown to Sally's apartment. I pulled up outside, nothing looked out of place. knocking on the door I got no answer. I tried again, calling her name as I did so. Nothing. I had her spare key, so I let myself in. Everything looked ok. Nothing out of place, just as she'd left it. She loved her job at the beauty salon so there should be no reason why she would just not bother turning in. I locked up the apartment and went back to my car. I decided to make my way over to the salon where she worked. Maybe I would spot her somewhere, having coffee with a friend. Wishful thinking.

Eventually I pulled up at the salon. I walked in and asked the girl on the desk if I could speak with Dana. She went and took over form Dana who was in the middle of washing some girl's hair.

"Hi, how can I help you?" she said as she walked over to me.

"Hi I'm Mike, we spoke on the phone earlier."

"Ah yes. Hi Mike, is Sally, ok?"

"I can't seem to find her. I've tried her phone a few times, and she's not answering. She's not at her apartment either." I said.

"Oh dear, I hope she's ok."

"Me too. Did Sally hang out with anyone from here?"

"Not sure about hanging out together, but her and Casey have been getting on really well lately, started walking to work together recently too."

"Does this, Casey live near Sally then?"

"Not too far away I don't think."

"Could you give me Casey's address?" I asked.

"Not sure I should be doing that."

"I just want to ask her if she might know where Sally is."

"I'll call her, she can tell us over the phone."

"Yes, that's fine. Thank you."

Dana pulled out her phone and tried calling Casey. No answer. This was becoming a bit of a habit today.

"She's not answering. I'll give you her address, but only because I'm getting a bit concerned with them both not answering their calls."

"Thanks, I appreciate it."

I parked my car on the road where Casey lives. As I walked to her apartment block, I was trying to think of what I would do next if she couldn't give me any answers.

Finally finding her apartment and knocking and calling at her door, there was no answer. What the hell was going on? I called Dana, told her Casey wasn't home and I would contact her again when I had something. At this point the only thing I could do, was go back home and see if Billy could get me some answers. I arrived back home, checked on the girls, then went to see Billy.

"Oh, hi Mike" he said, as I walked in the door.

"Morning mate. I need you to check something for me, if you have a minute."

"That I can do, what is it?"

"I need you to check Sally's phone records, see if she has spoken to anyone this morning."

"Ok, is everything alright?"

"Hope so mate. Not been able to get hold of her. She dropped the girls off to me this morning, so I could watch them while she was at work, only she didn't turn up for work. She's not at home, and she's not answering calls. Her phone keeps going straight to answerphone."

Billy was doing his usual key tapping and scrolling through his computer, looking at sentence after sentence of stuff only Billy could understand.

"Seeing nothing from this morning. There is a message that was received a few days ago from a number I can't get any information about."

"What did it say?"

"It said. YOU CAN'T HIDE AWAY FROM THIS."

"Is that all it said?"

"Yep. Nothing else"

Billy turned his screen so I could see for myself. It looked like the message had gone unanswered and deleted.

"She didn't reply?"

"It was just deleted, with no outgoing message."

"Ok mate. If you find anything else, let me know."

"Of course."

Making my way back to the main house, I couldn't help wondering of this had anything to do with those threatening calls she kept getting back in London. I hoped not. But I couldn't help thinking it.

I went back to see Danny and the girls.

"Everything ok mate?" said Danny.

"Not sure mate. Sally didn't turn up for work this morning, and she's not answering her phone."

"I'm sure there's a reasonable explanation."

"I have a bad feeling about this mate. When she was still in London, she had some threatening phone calls, to do with John's security firm. I guess somebody didn't like something he did. I may be thinking too much into it, but It's a feeling I can't shake."

"If there's anything I can do mate, let me know."

"Thanks mate. Billy has been checking her phone records, but has nothing yet."

We took the girls to the big dining room to get them some lunch. I wasn't that hungry but I managed to get a burger and a coffee down my neck.

"I think I might go back out and have a drive around. I know I'm probably not going to find her, but I feel better knowing I'm trying something."

"I understand mate. I'm coming with you."

We made sure the girls were settled again after lunch, then we went for a drive round.

4

Sally sat on a dirty mattress, in a dark room. One dimly lit lightbulb barely cutting through the darkness. Since being bundled into the back of a van, she hadn't spoken to anyone. She got pushed into this room and the door was locked. She had called out a few times but no answer came. Casey was not answering when she called for her. It was too dark in the room to see anything, so she just stayed where she was. She couldn't understand why this was happening, but she was more concerned about seeing the girls. Right now, she just wanted to hold them, but she knew they were in good hands. A voice came through the door...

"You can thank your husband for you being here. He messed up our plans with that security business of his. If he'd just pulled his men from that place like we asked him too, you wouldn't be here right now."

"My husband is dead. Who are you? What do you want?"

"Dead? Since when? We had a nice little robbery planned, and your husband's security guys messed it up. My boss didn't like that."

"My husband died over two years ago. Whatever happened to you back then was nothing to do with me."

"Well, this changes things. See, we took you so we could get what we wanted from your husband. It seems that we can no longer do that, so we will have to take it from you."

"Please. I don't have anything. Please, just let me go."

"That's not going to happen."

"Where is my friend?"

"She is sleeping right now."

"I want to speak with her."

"Hello?"

"Hello?"

No answer came.

5

Danny and I were driving around, mainly between Sally's apartment and her work place. What we expected to find, I didn't know. We'd been driving around for a couple of hours and I was starting to think we were wasting our time.

"Turn down this side road mate. We need to start looking down these alleys." Said Danny.

"Good idea. Although, if we find anything down one of these roads it probably won't be good."

"I don't like to say it mate, but you should maybe prepare yourself....."

"Yeah yeah, I know. Let's just try and think positive mate, hope we find something useful."

We spent another hour or so driving down little alleyways and side roads. There weren't many more little roads left to search when Danny told me to stop.

"Back up a bit mate."

I backed my car up a little way when he stopped me again.

"There."

He pointed down a little walkway, then jumped out of the car. I jumped out and followed him. He stopped halfway down and bent to pick something up. When he stood up and turned to face me, he was holding what looked like a smashed phone in his hands.

"Looks like an iPhone. Not entirely sure."

"I agree. Keep hold of it, we'll get billy to look into it. We need to search this area."

"I'll go up to this end. You take that end." Said Danny. We spent some time searching the little walk way, end to end. We met up again in the middle of the walkway. "Nothing mate."

"Nope. Let's get back to the car and take this phone to Billy." I said.

We walked back to the car but Danny stopped just short of getting in, and just stood there.

"You ok mate." I said.

He put his finger to his lips telling me to be quiet. That's when I heard it too. We could clearly hear a phone ringing.

"It's coming from the walkway."

We both walked slowly and quietly back down the walkway. We didn't get far before the ringing stopped. "Damn it." Said Danny.

"Just keep looking mate. We need to find that phone." That's when it started ringing again. We both turned to look back the way we had come. We had walked past it. We ran towards the ringing this time; we didn't want it to stop ringing before we found it. We came up to a pile of rubbish bags, and the sound was louder. We started throwing the bags aside as the ringing got louder. Then it stopped ringing.

"Keep looking mate, we know its here."

"Got it"

Danny held up the phone. It wasn't damaged so that was something.

"It's locked mate, so we can't look through it."

"Let's get back and get these to Billy. He will have it unlocked in no time. Hopefully he will be able to tell us something."

6

We arrived back at our place. We checked on the girls.
They asked where their mum was, so we just had to tell
them she was working late. Eventually we would have to
tell them the truth, but I just wanted to try and find out
all I could first. It was getting late in the day now so we
would have to tell them soon. Once we arrived at Billy's
den, he got straight on it.

"I'm not sure what I can do with this smashed one, that
may take a while, but I can certainly get into this other
one."

"Anything you can give us right now would be great." I
said.

"Ok, just give me another second... Voila. This one is
registered to one Casey Broomer."

"That's the girl from the beauty salon, it has to be. Her
boss said, her and Sally were getting pally."

"This phone just had a couple of missed calls when we
found it. Can you tell us who they were from?" asked
Danny.

"Yes. They were from... Dana. From someone called
Dana, both of the missed calls were from her." Said
Billy.

"That's the boss from the salon. She said that Sally and
Casey had started walking to work together recently.
This doesn't look good. If they were walking together

and both their phones were in the same area, then they both left that little alleyway together."

"If that other phone does belong to Sally, then we can assume there was a struggle of some kind, before they left that alleyway." Said Danny.

"Going by the state of the phone. I'd say you are right."

"Billy, I need you to get anything from these phones that may help. Anything. Let me know as soon as you have something."

"I'll get right on it."

"What do you plan on doing now, Mike?" said Danny.

"Not sure mate. We don't have much to go on right now. We can assume there was a struggle. Both Sally and Casey were taken somewhere, they had to have been. We really need something to come up on their phones."

"We should go back to where we found the phones, see if anyone saw anything."

"I agree mate, but you know what people are like these days. They won't admit to seeing anything."

"Then we should show a little cash around, maybe one of the rough sleepers may have a clue."

We drove back to the spot where we found the phones. There were a few rough sleepers dotted about in the area. I never really noticed them all the last time we were here, I was too focused on looking for clues.

"Where do we start." I said.

"We just split up and start talking to these people. Flash some money about. If they think we will pay for information someone may just give us something."
So that's what we did. We spent some time speaking to these homeless people, hoping at least one of them saw something. We just kept getting fobbed off. They didn't want to speak to us. One of the people I spoke to, got up and walked away. This was starting to feel like a waste of time. After speaking to a couple more people, I heard whistling behind me. I turned to see the guy who had stood up and walked, he was now peaking round the corner of a building waving me to follow him. Danny appeared at my side.

"Nothing mate. You get anything?"

"No, but that guy wants me to follow him."

"Let's go."

We walked towards the guy at the corner. As we got near, he started walking away again, so we just followed.

"You think he knows something?" said Danny.

"Don't know mate. We'll find out soon enough."

We continued to follow him through a labyrinth of, tents and little homemade sheds, that the homeless people had put together for some shelter. This was all situated underneath a highway flyover. It was damp and dark, and smelt like a rubbish tip. We continued to follow this guy out the other end of the area and round another corner, which took us to a concrete hut. It looked like it had housed electrical equipment at some point. Now it just had the odd wire poking from the walls and some make shift furniture. A good-sized guy was sat in an old threadbare armchair. He looked to well fed to be living out here.

"This must be the leader of the pack." Whispered Danny.

"I reckon."

"My man here, tells me you are asking questions and flashing money around. Do you think it's wise to do that round here? Likely get mugged if you ain't careful."

Me and Danny just looked at each other.

"Your man here, was right. We are asking questions. We are willing to pay for information that helps us."

"What is this information you are looking for?"

"We believe, two women were taken from this area this morning. Now, we are hoping someone from this area may have seen something that could help us find them."

"What exactly are you willing to pay for such information."

Danny took a step towards the guy in the chair.

"Listen to me. Cut the bullshit and tell us what you know."

I put a hand on Danny's shoulder to get him to cool it.

"Listen. If you know something then just tell us. I'll pay you and we can be on our way." I said with my hands up, showing him, we didn't want to make trouble.

"You need to rain in your pit-bull there" he said, pointing at Danny.

"I'm sorry about him, he doesn't like being pissed around." I handed him fifty dollars. "For you, to show no hard feelings."

The big guy in the chair looked at the money and smiled. Then he whistled. A few seconds later, a man walked into the hut and nodded at the big guy.

"Ok Terry. Tell them what you saw."

The new guy looked around unsure what to do. Then the big guy nodded at him.

"I was just sitting there minding my own business, and these two ladies came walking down our way. This ain't nothing unusual, but a car stopped at the end of the alley and just stayed there. I didn't pay much attention to it to start with. There were two beautiful ladies walking by, why would I worry about a car being there."

He looked at the big guy again. As if wanting permission to carry on. He received another nod.

"I was watching these girls walk by and I saw two men get out of the car at the end of the alley. They started walking towards the two ladies, I don't think the ladies noticed the men as they were too busy nattering. But then they got level with the men and that's when it got ugly."

"Ok mate. Just tell me what happened, could you hear them saying anything.?"

"I hid behind my trolley; I didn't want them to see me. I heard a name, John. Was a lot of shouting, then the men grabbed the ladies. One of them tried to use her phone, but one of the men grabbed it and stamped on it. I didn't see nothing after that. I just kept out of sight until they left."

"Can you describe the men?"

"One of em was tall and skinny. Long hair and a scruffy beard. Can't remember the other one."

"Did they take the ladies?" I asked.

"I didn't see, but when the car left the ladies were gone too."

"You didn't see the car's number plate?"

"No."

"Ok. Appreciate it." I said.

I handed the guy some cash, then we walked back to our car. We now knew that Sally and Casey had been taken. They spoke the name John. It couldn't be a coincidence, it was Sally. I knew it was.

We arrived back at our place. We went to see the girls first. I didn't know what to tell them, so I went with the truth. You can imagine their reaction to that, but I assured them I would find their mum and bring her home. It's a good job that Stan's house keepers are good with the girls. The girls love hanging out with them, which makes my life easier. We then went to see Billy.

"Billy, what do you have."

"Not much I'm afraid. I'm struggling to get anything from the smashed phone. And there isn't much to help us on the other one."

"We can pretty much confirm that the smashed phone is Sally's. The other one belongs to her colleague Casey."

"Well, I've managed to get into Sally's phone, but pulling anything useful from it, is proving difficult."

"I'm going to assume this has something to do with those threatening calls she kept getting back in London. I can't think of any reason anybody would take her. As for Casey, I think it's a case of, wrong place, wrong time."

"So, we say this is to do with the calls in London. Then we need to find the number those calls came from. Hopefully we can find an address for that number, then match the person at that address to the person described by the homeless guy earlier." Said Danny.

"Yes. Sounds simple when you put it like that."

"Look guys, I'll work on this until I get something. Why don't you go and get a drink or two? I'll let you know when I have something."

"Thanks mate. No matter what time it is, just let me know."

We made our way back up to the house. It was late now, but a couple of drinks seemed like a good idea. We walked into the big lounge room, and found Stan and Carol, sitting, enjoying some wine.

"Evening guys. Grab a drink and join us." Said Stan. "How's things going with Sally.?"

"Not great. Looks like she has been kidnapped, along with her friend. Billy is in the process of trying to get something from her phone, but it's been smashed pretty good so he's not holding out much hope."

"Anything I can do to help?"

"Not at the moment. But I'll be sure to let you know if anything changes."

"Yes, please do."

"So, How's it going with you two? You look pretty cosy." I said with a grin.

"Things are great here thanks." Stan said with a cheeky smile."

"Good. Glad to hear it." I said.

We'd been chatting for a good twenty minutes when my phone buzzed. It was Billy.

Danny and I said goodnight to Stan and Carol, then made our way to see Billy.

"What do you have for us Billy?"

"The computer is still working on the phone number from the threatening person, but I have some interesting photo's from the phone."

Billy brought up some pictures from the phone and put them on the large screen so we could get a better look.

"Ok gents, what you are looking at here are four pictures, all with different time stamps. Sally has obviously been taking photo's of everyday things, she'd obviously had her tourist head on when she took these. Anyway, I'm rabbiting on, take a look at this guy here."

Billy zoomed in slightly on a man in the background of one of the pictures.

"That looks like the guy our homeless man described." Said Danny.

"Then take a look at these other three photo's. He appears in the background of all four of these pictures. These pictures were taken within a three week period. He seems to be looking in her direction in every one of them."

"Makes me wonder if she knew he was there, and was just getting his picture. Or he was just watching her and she had no clue." I said.

"I'd go with the latter of the two." Said Billy.

"I'd agree with you but it's a coincidence him being there when she took those photo's."

"Well either way, I have his name. Say hello, to Garrod Potts. Fifty one years old, done a stint inside for drug trafficking and robbery. Grew up in New York. Currently owns property in New York and here in Los Angeles. My guess is they weren't legitimately brought. I have the addresses for the two properties. It looks like there were no hits on the phone number."

"My guess is that phone number would have belonged to Mr Potts, or an associate of his." Said Danny.

"I agree. Looks like we are going to be paying someone a visit."

"Lets get over to the L.A. address now. Billy, book us a flight to New York first thing in the morning."

"Consider it done."

"Billy, your a star."

It was getting close to midnight by this point. The address we were heading for was Griswold avenue, San Fernando. This was over to the East side of Los Angeles. The properties here were bungalow size properties. The streets were in a grid network. We found the property we were looking for and did a drive by to see if there was anyone around. We didn't see anyone, but there was a light on inside the property. So we parked along the road, close enough to see the property. Not too close as to be seen. We decided to watch the place for a short while, see if anyone came and went.

"What do you reckon our changes are on him being in there?" said Danny

"Well it's a fifty- fifty chance mate. If he isn't here, we'll be taking that flight to New York."

"We still don't know if he was the one who took Sally and Casey. If he was, he may well be elsewhere. If not, then I'm hoping he will tell us who did. You don't have to be here helping mate. I appreciate it, but you don't need to go travelling across country just for me." I said.

"You are like a brother to me Mike. If you need help, I'm there. Simple as that."

"Appreciate it mate." I said, as we fist pumped.

We'd given it nearly an our, so it was time to get in there. We left the car parked where it was, and went to the address on foot. When we got near, I told Danny to watch the back of the property as I went to the front. I knocked on the front door and waited. No answer. I knocked again, harder.

"Alright, alright leave the bloody door on the hinges will ya." Said a male voice as he unlocked the door.

"What do you want?" he said.

"I'm here to see Garrod."

"Garrod aint here."

"He told me to come see him if I wanted some good stuff."

"I don't know what good stuff you are talking about. Garrod aint here so get lost."

I put my foot in the doorway as he tried to shut it.

"Tell me where I can find him." I said.

"He's probably at one of his other places. Now remove your foot before I break it."

I removed my foot and let him slam the door shut. No point pushing it any more. If Garrod was in there he would have called him to come deal with me, rather that put up with the shit himself. I got Danny's attention and we went back to the car.

We sat there for another half hour, just to see if we'd made anyone want to leave the property all of a sudden. After that we went back home to get a bit of sleep before going to catch our flights in the morning.

10
0400 HRS
Manhattan New York

Garrod was fast asleep in his apartment on Lexington Avenue, when his phone started chirping. He looked at the clock then looked at his phone. "This better be important Frank." He said as he picked up his phone and answered the call.

"I wouldn't call you at this time if I didn't think it was important."

"Get to the bloody point man."

"Just had a guy here looking for you. He said you told him to come see you if he wanted some good stuff. He didn't look like the type to come looking for a score."

"Did he say anything else?"

"No. He just wanted to see you. I told him you weren't here and he got a little pushy, but left in the end."

"Did he have anyone with him?"

"Not that I saw. He came to the door alone. If this has something to do with those damn women, then I'm gone. You can run your own business. I can't afford to be caught up in this shit."

"Relax Frank. I've told you a hundred times, all we did was pick them up and take them to an address we were given. It's out of our hands now. The others can deal with them. I will sort this, you just get back to whatever you were doing, and leave it to me."

Garrod ended the call and laid there thinking about how to deal with this. It wasn't Franks problem or his. He knew he had to at least let the others know. He dialled a number he had memorized and waited for an answer.

"What do you want Garrod?" said the voice that answered.

"Frank just called me. Someone has been to the house looking for me. Frank thinks its more than just someone looking for a fix."

"Then deal with it. We don't have time for this bullshit. We have enough to deal with here."

"What do you want me to do about it? You told me all I had to do was get those two women to that address. My part is done." Said Garrod.

"Your part is done when I say its done. Now go deal with it."

The call ended. Garrod sat up in his bed, head in hands wondering what the hell he was going to do. He'd done what was asked of him, now it looked like he was in deeper than he thought.

Danny and I caught our Seven AM flight. We landed at JFK airport New York, around 5 hours later. It was now Three PM here in New York. We got through the airport and took a cab over to Manhattan. We didn't know if this Garrod fella was going to be there, but we didn't have much else to go on right now. I didn't like the fact that I had to keep palming the kids off back home, but I knew they were in safe hands. I just needed to get Sally back, then the girls would have their mum back. We had the cab driver drop us off a couple of blocks from the address we were heading to. Its always good practice to avoid any trace back to yourself, just in case the shit hit the fan. As far as the cab driver is concerned, we were a couple of blocks away, the last time he saw us. We went to get some food and something to drink. We weren't going to be knocking on Garrod's door until it was dark. Less chance of being noticed.

We spent a few hours, just walking around looking like tourists. When it finally got dark enough, we went to Garrod's apartment. It was on the fifth floor of the building, so we took the stairs. I asked Danny if he'd prefer to take the lift, but he told me to fuck off. I forget sometimes, just how easy he gets around on that prosthetic leg of his.

"Just hang back until the door is answered mate. Don't want him to feel threatened." I said.

I knocked on the apartment door and waited for an answer. I was surprised when the door was opened pretty much straight away.

"Can I help you?"

"Yes, I'm looking for Garrod."

"Who are you?"

"I'm Johnny, I've been told to see you if I want some good gear."

He looked a little quizzical, then opened the door. Danny walked up to me as I started in the door, and we both walked in together.

"Hey, who is this?" he said, pointing to Danny.

"This is a friend of mine. We just want to talk to you." I said.

"You said you wanted some gear."

"Are you Garrod?"

"I might be. What do you want?"

"We want to know what happened to a friend of ours."

"How am I supposed to know that. I don't know you."

He was starting to get fidgety now. I knew I was talking to Garrod.

"A friend of ours left for work yesterday morning, and hasn't been seen since. Neither has one of her colleagues."

"What's that have to do with me?"

I pulled out four photo's from my pocket and passed them to him.

"This friend of ours has been taking photo's recently and look who keeps appearing in them."

"Oh you think this is me? Looks nothing like me."

"We know its you. We know you are from New York. You also have a place in Los Angeles. You've done time for drug trafficking and robbery. We actually know a fair bit about you Garrod. Now cut the shit and tell us where our friend is."

Just then the bathroom door opened and a guy walked in pointing a gun in our direction.

12

EARLY HOURS OF THAT MORNING.

Garrod got out of bed and started pacing the room. He knew that this guy looking for him, would turn up here soon. He needed to end it there before this got out of hand. He phoned a couple of guys who helped him come up with a little plan to sort out this new problem.

"I'm telling you G, its the best way to sort this out fast." Said one of the guys.

"So I just let him in, then you shoot him?"

"Only if we need to. If he don't cause any trouble then he wont even know we are there. If he does start anything, we will make sure he leaves. Dead or alive."

"I don't know, seems a bit risky to me. Especially in my apartment." said Garrod.

"There will be hardly any mess, if any. We can dump the body, job done."

"I guess I don't really have any other option. I need him gone either way."

"Yes, exactly. I'll get over to you shortly. We can wait for him to turn up."

"No shooting unless absolutely necessary."
"Your the boss G. Your the boss."

13

We were told to sit down, so we sat on a small couch next to a coffee table.
"I guess we have the right man after all." I said to Danny.
"You called it." He said.
"Shut up talking. Looks like we have a slight problem now, doesn't it?
"Just tell us where our friend is and we'll be on our way." I said.
"You two need to sit there and shut up. I'm trying to think here." Said Garrod.
"This feels like Deja vu. Us sat together being threatened. Said Danny.
"It does mate. It's becoming a habit."
I leapt off the couch and dived at the guy with the gun. We went to the floor hard. I managed to get the gun from him, just to end up with another gun pushed into the side of my head.
"I suggest you get back in your seat." Said a second guy with a gun. Where the fuck did, he come from. I started

to stand up as he received a blow to his head. I turned to see Danny holding his prosthetic leg in his hands. I would have laughed had it not been for the fact that Garrod had somehow got hold of the gun I had taken from the first gun man. His first shot went wide, his second skimmed my thigh. By this point Danny had grabbed the other gun and put a couple of bullets into his chest.

"I guess we won't be getting any answers from him." I said.

"We will have to beat it out of these two." Said Danny. We got the guys sat on the couch.

"Let's do this the easy way guys. Tell us where our friend is and we are done here."

"We don't know where she is. We were told to grab her and take her to an address. That was the only part we played."

"Where did you take her? What's the address?"

"You're wasting your time; we took her and her friend to a warehouse and they were bundled into a van and taken away. We don't know where they are."

Danny and I looked at each other. It seemed to me that they were telling the truth. But that didn't help us.

"Ok, so you don't know where they are, but who told you to grab them? and who did you hand them over to?" said Danny.

"We don't know the guys we handed them over to. Never seen them before. We are just the foot soldiers;

we don't know where our orders come from. Were paid to do as were told, and that's all we do."

"You get your orders from someone. What's his name?"
They both looked at each other, not knowing how much to say. I think they realised they were better off giving us something.

"His name is Rico. Rico Cotes."

"Where can we find him?"

"You don't find Rico. He finds you. When he wants us to do something, he'll contact us or send someone with a message."

"You need to give me a bit more than that."

"We've seen him here in New York. He has a place in Bakersfield, north of L.A. That's all I know."

We tied them up with whatever we could find. They would get out soon, but it gave us time to get away from there. I contacted Billy and asked him to work his magic. He would get us what he could on this Rico guy. We left the apartment and went to find some food and a hotel. We didn't know where we were going from here.

14

Billy hated not being able to find information on people, but trying to find something on this Rico character was proving difficult. He managed to find a property in Bakersfield with connections to a Rico Cotes. It may not even be the same guy. There was nothing in New York for that name, so Bakersfield would have to be the starting point. He pulled up the most recent picture of the Rico he'd found, and sent it over to me with the address. That's when Stan walked in and asked how things were going.

"To be honest boss, not good. I've sent Mike what I have, but it isn't much. I'm not even sure I have the right guy."

"What do you have?" said Stan.

"An address in Bakersfield, and a picture of a Rico Cotes. If this isn't the right Rico, then were screwed."

"Give me the address, I'll send some guys over there. Tell Mike and Danny to stay put for now. Once we've checked out the address we can decide where to go from there."

Billy gave Stan the address and messaged me, telling us to stay put until they'd checked out this address. Stan went to round up some guys to go over to Bakersfield and see if they had the right Rico. He liked to make sure he sent enough men out on a job in-case there was any trouble. He sent four guys in two different vehicles, two men would check out the address, the other two would be standing bye near to the location.

It took the two vehicles just over an hour and a half to reach the address in Bakersfield. It was late evening there on the west side of the states. The address was in a reasonably quiet neighbourhood, so Stan's guys had to be careful not to cause a commotion. One of the vehicles pulled up a couple of streets away from the address. The other vehicle parked just down the street from the property they were going to. The property had no lights on, this could mean everyone was sleeping, or no one was in. Rob and John, the two guys who were going in first, had to be careful not to set any light sensors or alarms off. They were going to knock on the door and take it from there, but now the place was in darkness, they would have to go in silently. They both crept slowly around to the back yard, keeping tight to the wall and keeping an eye out for light sensors. They failed to spot one on the corner of the building and a bright light came on and lit up the back yard. They stopped moving and kept still, just watching and listening. A dog started to bark a few houses away, but that didn't last long. Rob took a piece of cloth that he carried on him for such occasions, and put it over the light sensor. Once the light went out, they would be able to move without setting the light off again. Once the light went out, they made their way to the back door. It's always worth trying a door or window before attempting to break in, they may just be unlocked. This time they weren't. The back door had four small window panes in the top half, that were just grouted into the door. John took a small suction cup from a kit in his pocket and stuck it to the pane of glass nearest the door handle. Rob then started to score the grout with a sharp knife while John kept hold of the suction cup. In no time the small pane of glass was out and no one heard a thing. There were no keys in the back door, but it had a turn handle lock, so Rob slipped his hand through the gap where the glass used to be, then slowly turned the small lock handle until he heard the door unlock. They both stood quietly for a few moments, just to make sure no one had heard anything. Once they were satisfied, they hadn't been heard, they moved in through the back door. They could see all the way down the hall towards the front door, they couldn't see any alarm keypads or flashing LEDs, so they had no reason to think there was an alarm in the house. They were wrong, kind of. As they stood in the kitchen area inside the back door, they suddenly heard growling. They both turned their heads to see a dog in the corner just standing there growling.

"Hello, shush now." Said John, trying to calm the dog down. He couldn't tell if it was a boy or not, or even what kind of dog it was, because of the darkness. But they needed to shut the dog up before it woke someone. John moved his hand slowly to a pouch on his belt, and pulled out a syringe. This did nothing to help calm the dog, it started growling louder. It managed to let out a bark as John lunged at it and stuck the syringe in it to put him to sleep. The dog went out like a light. It was a strong tranquilizer, but it would only last twenty minutes or so. An upstairs light came on and they heard footsteps across the floor upstairs. They both stood either side of the door and waited for whoever was going to come downstairs. It wasn't long before a tall man put his hand through the door and went to switch on the light. Rob grabbed him and wrestled him to the floor and just about managed to get him still enough so John could put him to sleep too. Once he was unconscious, they used zip ties to bound his wrists and ankles. Then they went to check if there was anyone else in the house. The down stairs rooms were clear and when they went upstairs, they heard a women say... "What's happening babe?"
She was shocked to see two men walk through her bedroom door. She didn't get a chance to scream because Rob was on her with his hand over her mouth

and in a sleeper hold. She was soon out cold. Rob and John put the man and the women in the living room downstairs. They sat them on the couch, tied up and gagged. They gagged the dog so it wouldn't make noise when it woke up. They made sure the curtains were all shut and switched on a small lamp in the corner of the room.

15

Bye the time Rob had notified Stan what had happened so far, the couple were starting to come around.
The guys waited for the couple to be fully awake and got their attention.
"I'm going to un tape your mouths, if one of you makes a noise I'll put you back to sleep, permanently. Nod if you understand."
The couple nodded.
Rob stepped close to them and pulled the tape from their mouths. John pulled out a Taser and made sure the couple saw it.
"We are going to ask you some questions. All you have to do is just answer. Understand?"
"The woman nodded. The man just sat there with a defiant look on his face.

"We aren't going to have any problems with you buddy, are we?" said Rob.

"We had problems the moment you broke into my house. What have you done with my dog?"

"Your dog is fine, it's just sleeping."

"Just tell us what you want, then get the fuck out of my house."

"Is your name Rico Cotes?"

"I think you already know my name, why else would you be here. You can see we don't have much worth stealing, but you obviously want something."

"Ok Mr Cotes. You gave an order for a woman to be taken off the streets and delivered to a warehouse, where she and her friend were bundled into a van and taken away."

"What the fuck are you talking about?"

John pulled out a picture of Garrod and showed it to Rico.

"Do you recognise this man?"

As soon as Rico saw the picture, Rob and John could both tell he knew him.

"Never seen him before."

"We know that's bullshit, Rico. Don't mess around. We know you gave the order. Where are the two women?"

"I don't know anything about any of that."

John walked over to the woman and gave her a shot with the Taser.

"You motherfucker, leave her alone." Said Rico.

"Tell us what we want to know and this stops"

"I've told you; I don't know."

The woman got another blast of electricity.

"You asshole. You will pay for this."

"We can do this all night. Don't worry, the next one will be for you. Don't want you feeling left out."

"Fuck you." Spat the man.

He got a longer blast than the woman did. It was her turn to have a go at us now.

"Leave him alone. He already told you, he doesn't know shit."

"Who do you work for?" said Rob.

"I don't work for anyone."

John went to zap him again but the woman spoke up, just in time.

"Reg. Reg alberson." She said, starting to sob. She knew she had fucked up, but she didn't want to see her man getting zapped. Rico gave her a dirty look.

"I'm sorry baby." She said. "I didn't want you to get hurt again."

"Shut up woman. Don't say another word."

She just put her head down and stared at the floor. Rob un tied the woman.

"If we need more information, we'll be back." He said.

They left, and let their buddies in the other vehicle know that they were heading back home. They contacted Stan and told him what happened, and gave him the name they had been told. He went straight down to see Billy.

Sally woke to her door being opened. She had a
headache and she felt really dehydrated.

"Hello, who's there?" she said with a hoarse voice.

"Just eat, you need to get your strength up." It was a
young sounding male voice.

"Why am I here? Please let me go."

"Just eat please."

"Where is my friend?"

The door shut again.

She crawled off the bed and made her way to where the
food was left. She still couldn't see too much because of
the darkness. She could see a dark silhouette on the floor
and felt a plate of what felt like bread, and some lumps
of cheese. Then feeling around some more she found a
bottle. After taking off the cap she gingerly testing to see
what it was, warm water greeted her lips. She gulped
down the contents of the bottle feeling the liquid going
through her. Picking up the bread and cheese, she put
them together and ate hungrily.

She was almost done eating when the door flew open
and Casey was dumped on the floor.

"What have you done to her?" she screamed.

Sally rushed over to Casey and held her. The door
slammed shut and left them in darkness once again.

"Casey, can you hear me?" Casey didn't answer.

"Casey?" she cuddled her. She could tell her breathing was short and shallow.

"What have they done to you?" she said, mainly to herself. Casey started to groan a little, but didn't move. Sally sat there rocking Casey in her arms and sobbing. She eventually got to her feet and started pounding on the door.

"We need medical attention in here! Hey, we need medical attention." She kept on banging on the door. "You bastards. Let us out" she screamed.

No one was listening. She carefully picked Casey up from the floor, with a struggle. She didn't have much energy but she wasn't leaving her on the floor. Finally, she managed to get her on the bed, where she cradled her in her arms and just laid there sobbing, until she drifted off to sleep.

17

"See what you can find on a Reg Alberson."
Billy got straight to work to see what he could find.
I'll call Mike, keep him in the loop." Said Stan.
"What do you have for us?" I said.
"I sent some guys over to that address and they got a
name. Billy is working on it as we speak."
"I'm guessing that Rico Cotes guy Isn't high up on the
food chain?"
"No. It was actually his girl who gave up this Reg
character."
"Let's hope he finds something useful. We haven't got
much else to go on."
"Something will come up. It has to. This Reg guy must
have a past."
"You'd think so."
"Boss. I have something." said Billy.
"Mike, I'll put you on speaker."
"Ok Billy, go ahead."
"Right, I have three Reg Alberson's that could be our
guy. One of them lives in Pittsburgh. One lives in San
Diego. The last one lives in a little place called Anglet,
in the south of France. They have all had dealings with
the police at some time in their lives. The Reg in
Pittsburgh seems the least likely, as he's been in the least
amount of shit with law enforcement. The other two are

pretty much similar as far as their criminal pasts go. I mean, they are all worth checking out."

"What was their criminal activity?" said Danny, who was listening in next to me.

"Reg in Pittsburgh was mainly getting in trouble for petty theft, and domestic abuse. He's slapped a few women about over the years."

"What an arsehole," said Danny.

"I couldn't agree more. Mr San Diego and Mr south of France, have been more into robberies, some armed. Violence seems to be their forte."

"Ok. We have three possibilities. What makes any of these three, want to kidnap two women off the street. Our guy is either doing this for himself, or he is doing this for someone else. Keep digging Billy, see if you can find something to tie one of these to sally or Casey. We'll get a few hours shut eye, then get back to you."

18

Sally woke to the door opening.

"Eat." Said the man who put the food tray on the floor.
He then backed out of the room and shut the door.

Sally took a few moments to wake up properly. Once she was with it, she looked over to Casey.

"Casey. Casey, wake up."

She got no answer. She nudged Casey to wake her, that's when she was hit by a big wave of fear. Casey felt cold and rigid.

"NO NO NO." She screamed as she cuddled Casey.

"It's my fault you were even here. I'm so so sorry." She sobbed and sobbed.

She shot off the bed and started hammering on the door. "You bastards. You will pay for this. Who do you think you are." She screamed at the door. She was banging and kicking the door, when it came ajar. She stopped. She didn't move. She wasn't sure if someone was about to come through the door. She stood there for a good couple of minutes. No noises, no one coming. She looked once more at Casey. "I'm so sorry." She said.

Looking through the tiny gap in the door she saw no one. Slowly, and as quietly as she could, she opened the door a little further. Was this a trick. Was someone out there waiting to beat her up too.

The door creaked ever so slightly but she just kept opening it, bit by bit.

Finally, the gap was wide enough for her to get through. She stood there for a moment wondering what was going to happen if she walked through the doorway. Was someone there waiting for her. Where was she even being held. Where will she go if she gets away. In the end she thought, screw it.

Slowly and as quietly as she could, she walked through the doorway. To her right was a boarded-up window. To her left was a dark damp hallway with two more doors. One was open, she could see the toilet, no one seemed to be in there. The other door was closed, she guessed it could be another bedroom. If it is, was there someone else being held in there. Then she realised that it was probably where Casey was being held. Her eyes welled up again at the thought of Casey lying there with the life beaten out of her. She had to pull herself together. There would be time for that later. Right now she needed to get out of there. She walked slowly passed the closed door and got to some stairs. There were no noises coming from down stairs. She laid on her stomach and tried to see if there was anybody down there. Not being able to see anything she stood back up and tried the first step. They were bare wooden stairs, and as she slowly put her foot on the step it creaked slightly. She slowly put more pressure on her foot and put all her weight on it. No more creaking. She painstakingly climbed down the first four or five stairs then stopped. She listened out for any noises and heard nothing. She carried on down the stairs until she reached the bottom. Again, she waited for any sign that there was anyone around. The house was eerily quiet. To her left was a long hallway leading to another closed door. There was a door half way along that was ajar. Straight ahead of her was the front door. The window in the top half of the door was boarded up, so she couldn't see anything on the other side. Slowly she walked towards the door, and went to grab the door handle. That's when he appeared.

19

After a few hours shut eye, Danny and I found a cafe for breakfast and coffee. I received a message from Billy, asking me to call him once I was sorted.

"Morning mate, what ya got for me."

"Morning Mike. I've been looking into these Reg characters and I came across a news article, talking about a foiled robbery a few years ago. After checking the story, I found the names of a couple of guys who were arrested for it. Now, these two guys were quick to give up there ring leader, but no one else was ever arrested. It seems that our San Diego Reg, is the one who was the ring leader. He denied knowing the two convicts, and somehow got away with his part. This all happened in the U.K.

Can you guess who foiled this robbery?"

"I'm going to go with, John's security firm."

"You are correct. It's safe to say, that the Reg in San Diego is the guy you want.

He is well connected. He has a lot of friends in high criminal places."

"This robbery must have been a big score, if it's led to Sally being taken because of it." I said.

"Oh yes, very big. It was an art gallery, said to hold the most valuable paintings in the whole of the U.K.

We are talking millions of pounds worth of art."

"That explains why Mr San Diego is angry about it, and not letting it go. Am I right in assuming, you have an address for this guy?"

"That I do. But while you are over on the East side, you should go to a little place called Harrisburg. Its around a Three hour drive from Manhattan. Our Reg has had properties there and some have been abandoned for whatever reason and left in disrepair. I can point you to the area where these properties are, but I can't get you an address."

"Ok. Send me everything you have. We'll check out Harrisburg, see if we can find anything there. Good work Billy. We'll be in touch."

Myself and Danny, set off for Harrisburg. We were a step closer to finding Sally, so that made me happy. Getting her home to her twins was the only thing I wanted in life right now.

We were going to do whatever it took to make that happen.

20

Sally froze. She stared at the man in front of her. She was frozen to the spot. Will he hurt her? What was about to happen?

"Wait here." whispered the man. He walked past Sally and went into one of the rooms. She didn't know whether to run out the door or just do as he said. He seemed nice for someone who had her held captive. She remained where she was, unable to move, unable to process what was happening.

The man returned.

"Ok we don't have long. We need to get you away from here before he wakes up."

"What? Who? Before who wakes up?"

"My brother. I slipped some sleeping pills in his coffee before I popped out."

He gave her, her shoes and a jacket. He then picked up a back pack from the side and checked the contents.

"Come on, follow me."

He led the way outside. They were in a cul-de-sac. There were 8 houses in this cul-de-sac and they were all empty. They looked like they had been abandoned. Gardens were overgrown. Windows were dirty. And there was a lot of rubbish just strewn about the place, on the pathways and in the gardens.

"You left my door open on purpose didn't you? Why are you helping me?"

"Because I've been doing bad things along with my brother for years. That's how we survive. But when we were told to bring two women here and hold them, I didn't like it. My brother beat your friend and left her there on the floor of her room. That was it for me. I swore I would get you away from him. I'm sorry about your friend, I swear I didn't do anything to her."

"Thank you for helping me."

"We just need to get away from here. If he catches us, we'll both end up like your friend."

"Why were we being held there? Why did he Kill my friend?"

"We were paid to pick you up and bring you here. We were told it was un finished business. Whatever it is you've done, you've really pissed of the boss man."

"Enough to make him do this to us?"

"He's killed people for less."

"What's your name." Asked Sally.

"Dennis."

"I'm Sally. Thanks again for helping me."

"Don't thank me, we haven't yet made it. We can't under estimate my brother. Once he wakes and realises, we have gone, he will be on the war path. He will have lots of people looking for us until we are found, then he will make us suffer."

"You are his brother, surely he wouldn't hurt you?"

"The only loyalty he has, is to the boss. He likes money and the boss pays him well for doing his dirty work."

"It's probably a good thing, you got away too."

"Let's just hope we do get away."

"Where are we?"

"We are in a place called Harrisburg. A two- or three-hour drive from New York city. That's where we will be heading."

"What's in New York?"

"Freedom. Hopefully."

21

We made it to Harrisburg around twelve noon. All we
had was a rough area where the properties were. No
actual address. We knew we were looking for some
derelict houses, but they could be anywhere in this town.
If Sally was here somewhere, we had to find her quick.
I've been on rescue missions in the past, and the people
you are looking for aren't always kept in one place.
Moving captives from place to place makes it harder for
rescue teams to find them, giving the kidnappers more
time to make plans. I was hoping Sally would still be
here somewhere. All we could do, was drive around and
keep looking.

We'd been driving around for a while when I saw a
vehicle drive past us. I would swear Sally was in the
passenger seat.

"Did you see that car?" I said to Danny.

"That old Toyota? Yeah, what about it?"

"I swear Sally was in the passenger seat."

"You sure?"

"Pretty damn sure." I said as I spun our car round.

"Why would she be riding around?"

"Don't know mate. Need to find out. Can't let that car
get away until we check."

"Let's hope we can catch up to it. Did you notice what model it was?"

"No mate. Didn't take much notice until I saw her."

"It was definitely a Toyota. Grey Toyota."

It didn't take us long to find the car. It was keeping to the speed limits, not wanting to draw any attention.

"Will keep back until we find a quiet bit of road, then make them stop." I said.

We followed from a distance, for about twenty minutes. We weren't going to get a better chance than this.

I put my foot down to get right up behind them, then flashed my lights until they pulled over to let me past. The car didn't pull over. I kept flashing at the Toyota, but the driver was not going to let me bye.

"I'm gonna get this license plate to Billy, he may be able to get us the owner." Said Danny.

He called Billy and gave him the license plate number. It wasn't long before he had a name for us.

"Dennis Fulburn, is the owner of that vehicle. Grey, Toyota Camry."

"Do you have an address for him?"

"He has an address in Manhattan."

"He's heading in the New York direction. Send us the address, we may need it."

"Will do. Good luck guys."

I was still struggling to get alongside the Toyota. I needed to confirm that it was Sally in that car.

"I'm going to have to nudge him." I said.

"Just do it in a place where they can't smash into something." Said Danny.

"There's a bit of open road coming up, just fields on either side. That's our best chance."

"You better make it count."

We went a little further, then came out of the built-up area into some countryside.

"Brace yourself mate."

"Go for it."

I put my foot down and gave his bumper a knock. He wobbled a bit but kept control.

"Damn it. Gonna try again."

I tried to nudge him again, but he was ready and swerved away. I lined up for another try and he braked hard, causing me to scrape along the side of him. That was definitely Sally in that car. She looked over and towards us and I could see the shock on her face. Probably wondering what we were doing there and why we were trying to ram them off the road. I could see her shouting at the driver. It looked like she was trying to tell him to pull over and he was shouting back. I tried to knock him side on but he sped up again. We were still side by side, so I went for it again. He braked hard, so I ended up turning in front of him and into the field. I tried to keep the car going but it lost traction and we stopped. We were stuck.

"Son of a bitch."

Now I was pissed off. We almost had them, so close to getting her back.

"Better call a tow truck."

22

Sally was not happy. She was shouting at Dennis.

"You just ran our only chance of help, off the road. I told you they were my friends."

"Right now, we have no friends. We can't trust anyone right now."

"Stop this damn car and let me out!" she shouted.

"I'm not stopping this car until we get to where we are going."

"Those men are my friends. They've obviously been looking for me. Just turn around and go back. They can help us."

"They can't help us. We can only help ourselves. We aren't stopping until we get to New York."

"I wouldn't want to be you when they catch up with us, and trust me, they will catch up with us."

"We will have enough people looking for us soon. Two more won't make any difference. Besides, they won't find us where we are going."

"You helped me escape from your brother just to keep me held somewhere else?"

"I won't be holding you there. I'll be keeping you safe."

"The only way to keep me safe, is to take me back to my friends."

"Not going to happen."

Sally gave up shouting and just sat there staring out of the window.

23

Me and Danny stood at the side of the road, waiting for a tow truck.

"Mate, we need to find them. we don't know where that guy is taking her." Said Danny.

"I know mate. Billy has the car info, so hopefully he can trace it when we get going. I'll ring him."

"What do ya need Mike?"

"Billy. Mate, can you track that Toyota?"

"You lose them?"

"Something like that. Slippery bastard."

"I will see what I can do. I was able to trace it earlier, so I should be able to track it. Will take a while though."

"Ok mate. We have a little time now anyway. Tow truck is on its way. See what you can do buddy."

"Will do. I'll call you the second I have something."

The tow truck turned up eventually. After spending an hour nearly, pulling my car from the ditch, the truck driver left us to it.

We set off in the New York direction. We didn't know if the driver was taking Sally to New York, but we could only assume at this point. We travelled for an hour maybe, when Billy called.

"Give me some good news Billy."

"Good news is, I can trace the licence plate. Bad news is, I can't see it in real time. All I can do is give you an area where they are, then you will have to find them."

"Ok mate. That's better than nothing. Appreciate it. Where is the car now?"

"I last had them in the Morristown area. A couple of hours drive from Harrisburg, and about an hour from Manhattan."

"They have a good hour or so on us. We will need to put our foot down to stand any chance of catching them up."

"I'll keep an eye on them. When you get to Manhattan, I'll update you on their last location. I won't be able to pin point it though."

"Ok mate. We'll call when we get there."

We kept driving faster than we should have been. We risked being pulled over, but we needed to get to Manhattan sooner rather than later.

Eventually we crossed the river into Manhattan. Danny called Billy to get a location for Sally.

"I have the vehicle in Brooklyn Downtown area. Like I said, it's not real time. That's the last location I can find them in. They may still be in the area."

"We will look around. If the location changes, let us know."

"Will do."

All we could do now was drive to Brooklyn, and see if we can find them. As long as they don't leave the area, we had every chance of finding them.

24

Dennis pulled his Toyota up outside the door of a run-down industrial building on Hall Street. This area was a small industrial area on the west side of Brooklyn. He escorted Sally from the car to the door. He unlocked the old metal door and they entered. Dennis locked the door behind them. He ushered her through the building, through some old storage rooms and some old offices. They climbed three stair cases and ended up at another metal door. He unlocked the door and they walked in. Sally was not expecting to see this apartment in amongst these old run-down spaces. The rooms and offices they passed on the way to the apartment were all derelict. This was an open plan apartment. No carpets. Windows covered with different coloured sheets instead of curtains. A little kitchenette in one corner. Toilet and shower in a small room in another corner. And two threadbare sofas sat either side of an old metal coffee table.

"Why is this place even here?" asked Sally.

"I use it when I want to keep out of the way. It's my safe place."

"Does your brother know this is here?"

"Nobody knows. You are the only other person who now knows about it."

"How long are we going to stay here?"

"As long as it takes to figure all of this out. We are not safe. My brother will come looking for us. If he finds us, he will kill you, and make me suffer."

"Then let me call my friends. Trust me, they are our best chance of dealing with this."

"We can't trust anyone right now. We will figure this out, then you will be free to go."

"Just let me go now. You are safe here; I'll take my chances with my friends."

"I hate to say it, but you are my leverage. If I let you go, I will have nothing to bargain with."

"Bargain with? What do you mean?"

"I mean, if your friends, or my brother turn up."

"You mean, trade me in to free yourself? You help me escape, then hold me here for yourself. You are no better than your brother."

"I'm nothing like my brother! I helped you so we could both get away. I do not plan to hurt you. I may just need you to buy myself some time. Then you are free to go."

"So, you use me as some kind of bait, then run away?"

"That's not what I meant."

Dennis's cell phone started to ring. He looked at it and saw it was his brother calling.

"Shit"

"What? Who is it?"

"Michael. My brother."

"You going to answer it?"

"No."

The phone stopped ringing. A few seconds later it started again.

"Maybe you should answer it."

"Keep quiet."

"Hello."

"Don't fucking hello me. Where are you?"

"Doesn't matter where I am."

"Is that little bitch with you?"

"I am by myself"

"Don't fuck me about Den. You better bring her back here. If the boss finds out what you've done, he won't be happy."

"Fuck the boss. I've had enough of this. When did we start killing people? That's not our job, Michael."

"Jobs change Den. We just do as we are asked and get paid. Simple as that."

"No. Not anymore."

"You know I will come and find you. Don't make me hurt my own brother."

"You don't have to. We could find another job, a normal job like normal people. No more illegal shit."

"You are talking out of your arse Dennis. What is wrong with you? You need to get back here, and bring her with you."

"Not going to happen. You won't find me. She has friends who are looking for her. So, you aren't the only one who wants her back. She is better off with me right now."

Michael laughed when he heard this.

"Dennis, you are afraid of your own shadow. You can't protect her, and you know it."

"I can. I will."

"You leave me no choice Den. When I find you, I will kill you both!"

"You don't even know where I am. Good luck with that."

Dennis ended the call. He dropped his phone on the floor and smashed it. He threw the pieces into the fire place and got the fire going.

"We are safe here." He said. "Why don't you get some rest."

"Did you get it?" said Michael.

"Yes boss. They are in a little industrial area in Brooklyn."

"I knew that tracker would come in handy one day."

"The phone tracker signal is down."

"He isn't as stupid as we thought. We still got the signal from the car?"

"Yes boss."

"Good. Gather up some men. We are going for a drive."

"Yes boss. How many?"

"Three guys and the two of us will do. One vehicle attracts less attention."

"On it boss."

Michael was rather calm, considering his brother just took away his payday. He loved his brother but would not hesitate to kill him, if that's what was needed.

If he had to kill his brother to get the girl back, then so be it. It was his head, if he didn't get her back. The boss wants her for whatever reason, so he would deliver. No matter what. His men got organised, then they set off on a trip he was not looking forward to.

We arrived in Brooklyn. All we could do was drive around hoping we would see the grey Toyota.

"We need to call Billy. See if he has an update."

"I'll call him now. Keep your eyes peeled for that car."

"Billy, you have anything new?"

"The Toyota is still in Brooklyn. Looks like a different location. It's a small industrial area on the west side. I'll send you the address."

"Cheer's mate."

The call ended and Billy sent me the address.

"We want, Hall Street. Little industrial area."

"Let's hope he hasn't hidden the car. This will take all night if he has."

"We will find out soon enough."

It took us about fifteen minutes to get to hall street.

It was a long street, just houses and no industrial units.

"Let's drive down to the end mate, see if we find it."

We drove down the length of Hall Street, not seeing any industrial places. We were almost at the end of the street when we saw a few old looking industrial buildings.

What was more interesting, was the grey Toyota parked outside one of them.

"Got ya." I said. "Park out of sight mate."

We found a spot away from the building and parked the car.

"The Toyota is parked outside that door. Seems like a good place to start."

"Something's not right, Mike. Why would he just leave the car out in the open like that? It's like, he wants us to find it."

"Yeah, I know what you mean mate. Seems a bit odd. Try the door, take it from there."

"Let's just stay away from the car."

"Agreed."

We tried the metal door. As expected, it was locked. We decided to look around the building for another way in. The windows in the front of the building were too high, so we walked around the back. None of the windows were reachable from the floor, so we looked for something to pry open the back door. We eventually found some bits of metal scaffolding, and some scrap lying around. We spent some time trying to pry open the door, not knowing if they were even in this building. We eventually gave up trying to break the door open and decided to stack some old pallets and oil barrels up to get to the window. Finally, we were in. Luckily for us these windows weren't metal strengthened, or we would have had problems.

"Take it steady mate, we don't know if they are in here, or if he has set some traps for us." I said.

"We both know what happened last time we walked into a trap." Said Danny, referring to the time we went into a house to catch someone and he got his leg blown off.

"We do mate, but you can almost out run me with that bionic leg of yours."

"Not quite bionic, but it's pretty cool I must admit."

We both chuckled. Danny never let the loss of his leg get to him. He was happy with the prosthetic Stan had, had made for him. He would joke about it as much as the rest of us.

We walked carefully through the first floor of the building, checking each room as we went. We would check the whole building before moving on.

After clearing the first floor we moved up the stairs to the second, watching our backs as we went.

We did this for three floors. As we climbed our third set of stairs, we came to a landing with another metal door. There were more stairs leading up to the next floor, but that could wait, we needed to check behind this door before moving on.

"I say we just knock"

"Why not." I said.

Danny knocked hard on the metal door. We waited for a few moments, nothing.

"I don't think he is just going to open up." I said.

"You still got that gun, you got from Garrod's place?"

"Yes mate."

I pulled the weapon from my waist band to show him.

"I say we knock again, then put a couple of rounds into that lock."

"Ok go for it."

Danny and I both hammered on the door, calling out to Sally. Then we thought we heard voices.

27

Dennis and Sally were resting. Both lying on one of the sofas. A coffee table separating them.

Suddenly there was a loud banging noise. They both sat bolt upright, startled by the loud noise.

Dennis put his finger to his lip, indicating to Sally to keep quiet. He walked over near the door and listened for any clues to who it was. No one knew this place was here. Why was there someone banging on the door. He realised it couldn't be his brother, because he was too far away to get here this quick, and he didn't know about this place either. Then there was more banging. Lots of banging and calling out for Sally. This got her attention.

"That's my friends, let them in they can help."

"sssshhhhh" he said.

"Just open the damn door, Dennis. Listen to me. They won't hurt us; they are my friends."

"Just be quiet." Said Dennis.

"MIKE." Sally shouted. She wasn't letting them get away again. "MIKE HELP ME."

Dennis ran over to Sally and slapped her across the face. "Shut up I said."

She fell back on to the sofa, holding her face.

The next noise they heard, was the sound of a gun being fired at the door.

Dennis grabbed Sally, stood behind her and put a knife to her throat.

"Dennis, you don't have to do this."

"I'm sorry for hitting you. Please just be quiet."

There was more banging coming from the door. After a few more bangs the door started to rattle, then it flew inward, followed by two men.

28

The sight I saw when we got through that door, made my blood boil. The driver of the Toyota had a knife to Sally's throat. I raised my gun, and aimed at his head. "Let her go." I said.

Danny walked round to the side of the room to get a better angle.

"Don't come any closer." Dennis warned Danny.

"Look mate, just let her go and we can talk about this." Danny knew that sounded lame as soon as it came out of his mouth.

"Look man, we are here to take our friend back. No harm will to come to you. Just put the knife down."

"If I put this knife down, he will shoot me. Who are you?"

"My name is Danny, this is Mike. We are here to help. Whatever you've done, I'm sure we can sort it out."

"Dennis, please listen to them. They are here to help. They can help you too." Said Sally.

"We've come all this way to escape my brother, just to hand ourselves over to these two?"

"Dennis, these are good guys. Please, just let me go."

"It sounds to me, like you've helped Sally. Let her go then we can all work together to sort this out." I said.

Dennis looked from Myself, to Danny. He seemed to be thinking about what we were saying.

"Come on mate, don't make me shoot you. If you hurt her, you are going down. Do you understand me?"

Dennis looked between us again. After a few seconds, he slowly pulled the knife away from Sally's throat. Sally ran over to me and threw her arms around me sobbing. The sobs were more for relief than anything else.

Danny walked over to Dennis and took the knife away from him. "Sit down mate" he told Dennis.

Dennis backed away and sat down on one of the sofas. I sat Sally on the other sofa, then put the gun away and walked over to Dennis and punched him hard in the face. Danny ran over and pulled me away before I did it again.

"Calm it mate. Let's hear what he has to say."

"Guys, listen to me," said Sally. "Dennis helped me escape. He has done nothing to hurt me. He didn't like the fact that his brother hurt Casey, so he helped me get away."

"Where is Casey now?" I asked.

"She's dead." Sally's eyes started tearing up again. "She died in my arms Mike. That bastard beat her so bad."

"Your brother?" I asked, pointing to Dennis.

"Yes, unfortunately. What he did was horrible, I couldn't let him do that to Sally."

"Where is this brother of yours, now?"

"Probably out trying to find me. How exactly did you two find us anyway?"

"I guess you didn't know about the tracker then?"

"I smashed my phone. That can't be tracked now."

"The tracker we followed, is in your car."

"No fucking way. That son of a bitch."

"You need to get rid of that car. Take it somewhere out of the way and burn it."

"I will. As soon as I've cleaned myself up."

"Don't expect an apology for that bloody nose." I said.

"I don't. Will you all still be here when I get back?"

"We are taking Sally home. You can sort out your own mess."

"It's not that simple. My brother will do what it takes to please his boss. That means getting her back."

"What do they want her for?"

"Our boss, well my brothers' boss, says that Sally's husband stopped a robbery a few years ago, which cost him dearly. Now he wants payback. He now knows that her husband is dead and wants to take revenge on her. He's already made sure her friend was killed."

"So, we need to stop your brother now, too?"

"He will keep going until he finds her, us. I can help you stop my brother, but you have to be here when I get back. I will go with you."

"You have thirty minutes to get that car away from here and destroy it. We leave here in thirty minutes, with or without you."

29

Michael Fulburn was on his way to Brooklyn.

He had organised for a couple of guys who lived in
Manhattan, to go over to the address where the car was
parked. He thought they could get to Dennis first and
hold him and Sally there until he arrived.

As the two guys got to the address, they saw Dennis get
into the car and drive away.

"I think we should follow him." Said one of the guys.

"I think he was on his own. That means he left the girl in
that building somewhere."

"We can't risk the chance. If we lose him and the girl
isn't in the building we are screwed."

"Ok, we'll follow."

Dennis knew of a small piece of wasteland on the edge
of the east river. It was a perfect place to take the car and
burn it. Even in broad daylight. He would then walk a
couple of blocks and pick up a cab back to the
apartment.

After arriving at the piece of wasteland, he pulled the car
in and tucked it to one side out of view of the main road.
He got out of the car, ready to light it up and get away
but he noticed a gap in the fence on the river side of the
area. He then had an idea. He got back in the car and
drove it through the gap and onto a thin strip of pebbles
leading down to the river. With the car still rolling

slowly, he got out and pushed to help it the rest of the way. He then watched as the car went onto the water and stayed there until it sank.

The two guys who were following him, saw him go into the small wasteland area and they pulled up along the road and waited. They soon saw Dennis leave the area and walk away. They watched him walk a couple of blocks then get in a cab, so they followed. It wasn't long before the cab dropped Dennis off outside the apartment. The two guys watched him unlock the metal door and go in. After a few moments they got out of their vehicle and walked to the metal door and tried to open it.
"We aren't getting in here very easily. We will just have to wait. We can keep an eye out, make sure he doesn't leave with the girl, and wait for Michael to get here."

Dennis climbed the stairs back up to the apartment. Once he got there, he didn't have to worry about unlocking the door because it was still hanging off its hinges.
"We may have a problem guys." Dennis said as he walked through the doorway.
"What's wrong?" Said Danny.
"I disposed of the car. Once I left the area where I disposed of it, I noticed a vehicle parked nearby. I got into the cab that brought me here and they followed. They are parked along the road."
"Did you recognise them?"

"No. Two biggish men in the vehicle. It's a dark blue Escalade."

"Nothing to do with your brother then?"

"They could be. He has a lot of men working for him."

"What shall we do?" asked Sally.

"I think we should get them inside this building. We can deal with them off the street then." Said Danny.

"Ok, we need a reason for opening that metal door."

"Trash. Take a trash bag out the main door and when you come back in, forget to shut it properly. We can then wait for them to come in. If they are watching, they will come in."

"Let's hope they are dumb enough not to see it as a trap."

"If they are watching Dennis, the chances are they think its only him and possibly Sally here."

"So much for nobody knowing this place was here." Said Sally.

Dennis just shook his head and walked over to the trash can and pulled out the trash bag. He walked out of the apartment and down to the main door. Danny, Sally and myself followed and found a good hiding spot. Once Dennis had taken out the trash bag, he came back through the door and left it slightly ajar.

"Let's hope this works." He said, as he found a hiding place for himself.

"Look." Said one of the guys.

Both men looked at the building as Dennis came out carrying a trash bag. He dumped it outside the door and went back in.

"He hasn't shut the door; this could be our chance."

"Let's just wait a few minutes, make sure he doesn't come back to shut it."

They waited and watched for ten minutes before deciding that Dennis wasn't coming back to shut the door.

"Ok let's go. We sneak in quietly, take them by surprise."

The two men got out of the vehicle and walked over to the metal door. One of them opened the door a fraction so he could take a peek inside. He saw nothing but scattered old furniture and empty space.

He gave his mate the nod and he opened the door and walked in.

30

Once both men were inside the building they looked around and noticed the stairs. they were about to head towards them when they heard a noise from across the room.

We watched the two men come through the door. They were looking towards the stairs when I moved my foot and knocked over a piece of wood that was leaning against the wall I was next to. We had to make our move.

I stood up, bringing my gun up from my waistband at the same time. Danny stood up next to me and Sally kept down. The two guys looked shocked to see us appear like that, especially when they recognised us from Garrod's place. One of them had his gun pointing in our direction.

"You two again. Interfering in business that doesn't concern you."

"Oh, this concerns us very much, that's why we are here." I said.

"Our boss will be here soon; he doesn't take kindly to people interfering in his business. Where is the girl?"

"The girl isn't going anywhere with you. You can tell your boss to back off. Whatever his problem is, he needs to let it go."

"Right now, you are his problem. You got lucky last time we met; you won't be so lucky this time."

This was the moment Dennis stepped out from his hiding place and held a knife across the throat of the other guy.

"Put the gun down. I should have known it was you two."

The guy with the gun, turned to see his mate standing there with a knife to his throat.

"Dennis, what the fuck are you doing?" said the guy with the gun.

"Just put the gun down John. My patience is starting to run out."

The guy slowly bent down and placed his gun on the floor. "Your brother will be here soon. What do you think he will say about all this?"

"I don't give a shit about my brother right now, or what he has to say."

"Step away from the gun." I said.

The guy stepped away from the weapon and Dennis pushed his mate to stand next to him.

"Looks like we got lucky, again." Said Danny.

"Your luck will run out soon enough. I don't think you realise, just how much shit you are in right now."

"We always seem to get out of the shit, one way or another." I said.

"Cocky bastard." Said the guy's mate.

Sally popped up from her hiding spot.

"We need to get out of here Mike." She said.

"Let's get these two upstairs. Get them secured, then we get out of here." I said.

"Don't you think we should finish this. Deal with my brother when he gets here. He won't stop looking for us if we don't." Said Dennis.

"He has a point," said Danny. "If we leave now, we still have to deal with this. Sally won't be safe. I think we should stay and sort this out."

"Let's just get out of here. They won't mess with me now, not when you've shown, you won't let them." Said Sally.

"No, they are right. We need to stop this now. We don't know what these people are capable of. Besides, we don't even know where the mastermind is yet. We need to find that Reg character. That's where we need to stop it." I said.

Everyone, apart from Sally, agreed to making a stand here. we steered the two guys in the direction of the stairs, to take them up to the apartment out of the way. We didn't get far, before one of the guys tried his luck. He spun round, knocking the weapon from my hand. That's when it all went to shit.

I grabbed one of his arms to try and take him down. I struggled as he was a strong son of a bitch. While we were having our tussle, his mate went for Danny. He didn't fare too well, as Danny was a strong fucker too. These guys were easy to deal with last time, when we had a gun pointing at them, this time they had nothing to lose and weren't holding back.

An elbow to my face was the next thing, which felt like being hit with a lump of concrete. This guy was tough and he was going to get the better of me if I wasn't careful. Another blow came towards me but I managed to avoid that one. I caught that one under my arm pit, clamped his arm there, and started pounding his ribs. To start with, it seemed like he wasn't feeling the blows, but after four or five hits he started to moan out in pain. I was finally starting to get somewhere, or so I thought. A couple more punches to his ribs, then he yanked his arm free and dived at me. By this point, we were only two stairs up from the first landing, so we didn't fall far. We hit the concrete landing together, side by side. he dealt with it well, I was winded. I struggled to get my breath, but had no time to recover. He was on me again, pounding away, like he was trying to punch me through the landing. All I could do was curl up and protect myself as best I could. This guy was enjoying some payback.

Danny had his guy down, and was just holding him there out of the way.

Dennis was next to join in. He dived on top of the guy that was pounding on me, and started to strangle him. The punches didn't stop straight away, but soon enough he slowed down and the punches got weaker. Dennis had him in a sleeper hold, and was squeezing with all his strength to slow this guy down. The guy was nearly out when I stopped Dennis.

"Ok mate, let him go, or we'll have to carry the fucker up the stairs."

Dennis let go and the guy rolled off and laid there catching his breath.

31

We finally got the two guys up to the apartment. Dennis followed us up after making sure the main door was locked. It wouldn't be long before his brother turned up. None of us knew what would happen when he did. The heavy locked door would give us time to figure things out. We tied the two guys up. I then went to clean myself up.

I was getting evil looks from the tough guy.

"You should be used to being tied up by now." I said with a smile.

"Fuck you." Is all he had to say.

One of the guy's phones started chirping. Dennis looked at me. "Just ignore it" I said. "It's probably just their boss, or your brother."

I walked over to Dennis and said "Thanks for helping out back there. Sorry for giving you a bloody nose."

"And I thought I wasn't getting an apology for that" he said, smiling. "I'm sorry for being part of the kidnapping. If I'd known what my brother was going to do, I wouldn't have had any part in it."

"If you hadn't had any part in it, Sally may not have got away."

"Call it even then." He said with a smile. Then we just shook hands.

"Guys, I think we have visitors." Said Sally.

We walked over to the window she was looking through, and saw an SUV pull up in the street below.

"That's one of my brother's vehicles." Said Dennis.

A few seconds later, another SUV pulled up next to the first one. The windows were rolled down and the occupants from both vehicles were talking to each other. We couldn't see any faces from up here, but we could imagine what was being said.

32

Michael had his driver pull up on the street where Dennis's trace was recorded.

"Try those two goons again, they should be answering their damn phones."

"Nothing boss. I've tried a few times, they aren't answering."

"Keep trying. They should have it all secure in there." Michael wasn't a patient man. If things didn't go his way, everyone would know how pissed off he was.

Just then, another SUV pulled up alongside his vehicle. He rolled down the window, as did the passenger in the other vehicle.

"Bobby, you need to get hold of your boys, they aren't answering their damn phones."

"Relax Mikey. I'm sure they have it all under control."

"I'll relax when that fucking girl is back here with me. Reg wants her over at his place. That takes a few days as it is, we don't have time to fuck around. If I don't get paid, you fuckers don't get paid."

Bobby was used to Michael having a go at him. He had worked for Reg for years and he knew Michael was one of his most loyal guys. He was older than all of the guy's Reg had working for him. He just took things in his stride. He was getting too old to get stressed over things he had no control over. He just let Michael get it out of his system. Johnny and Bobby Jnr, were his boys. He knew they would have everything in hand and waiting for them to turn up.

"I'm assuming this is the building where his car was?"

"This was where we picked up the trace originally. We now know he dumped the car, after our wasted trip to that piece of wasteland. He was obviously trying to throw us off."

"What makes you think he is still in there?"

"All we have, is the last known location before he dumped the car. They are in there; I know they are."

Michael trusted his gut; it was right most of the time. Bobby trusted it too.

"Let's do this, before I get even older." Said Bobby.

Four guys from both SUVs got out of the vehicles and walked over to the metal door. They had crowbars with them, and started to work the door.

Bobby sent a couple of his guys round the back of the building to look for another way in.

33

I knew it wouldn't be long before they found a way in, so we needed to do something.

"We are outnumbered. We can't take them all on. We need to get out of here." I said.

"Agreed." Said Danny.

We made sure the two guys weren't going to get out and cause us more problems. Dennis grabbed a few things that he needed, then we made our way down the stairs.

"We should go out the way we came in, then we can get back to our car without being seen." Said Danny.

"Makes sense." I said.

We made our way down to where we made our way in. before we got there, we saw someone climbing in through the window we had previously used. Once he was inside, another guy followed him in.

"Shit. We need to take them down before they go and let the others in." I whispered.

"Sally, you wait here. Don't make a sound." Said Danny.

Myself, Dennis and Danny, walked slowly towards the two men and got quite close before they realised, we were there, and spun round to react. These guys weren't quick enough. Dennis and myself, dived at the nearest guy, and Danny ran at the other one. This fight was over before it even started. Both men were rendered unconscious within a few seconds.

"Grab their phones, and weapons if they have any." I said.

I went to get Sally and we all met back at the window. "Danny goes first, you two follow him. Stay low and stay quiet once we are outside."

Danny climbed through the window and lowered himself down onto the makeshift platform we had made earlier when we climbed in.

Once we were all outside, we quietly made our way towards the car. When we reached the car, we heard shouts coming from along the street.

"There they are." Someone shouted.

"Get in the car" I shouted. "Go go go."

We all dived in the car and I got it started. I backed the vehicle out from where it was parked and we started taking gun fire. "Shit." I shouted. I rammed the car into drive and floored it. We came to a bend at the end of the street and we drifted round it sideways. I needed to put some distance between us. I didn't know these streets, but I wasn't slowing down. Left right, left right, I just kept making turn after turn to make it more difficult for them to follow. If they were chasing after us, I wasn't going to make it easy.

"Danny, call Billy. He needs to get us out of here."

"Hi Danny, how's it going?" said Billy.

"We've been shot at, and are now probably being hunted. We need to get back."

"Danny, it's Stan. Did you get Sally?"

"Yes boss. We have an extra one here with us too."

"Well, that's good news at least. You need to head in this direction. I'm sending out our helicopter to get you. The further you make it this way the better. You may have to find somewhere to lay low over night."

"Did you say, helicopter? Since when do we have a helicopter." Said Danny.

"I decided to get one after we blew Rufus's helicopter to bits. Haven't had the pleasure of taking a flight in it yet. Anyway, keep travelling this way, we will arrange a pick-up area, and get you all back home."

"Will do. Will call you first thing in the morning." The call ended.

"We need to find somewhere to hide out overnight. We will be picked up in the morning. Just keep heading in the direction of home, until we find somewhere suitable."

"Did I hear you mention a helicopter?" I asked.

"Yeah. Stan's new toy, apparently.

34

Michael was losing his shit. First, he wasn't getting any answers from bobby's boys. Now he'd lost Dennis. "Somebody please tell me they got the fucking license plate number."

"Yes boss."

"You lot, go after them." Said Michael, pointing to some of his men. Three of his men jumped into one of the SUV's and set off to give chase.

"Those fucking boys of yours were meant to hold them here until we arrived."

"I'm sure there's a good explanation for all this." Said Bobby.

"Being dead is the only explanation for letting them get away. Bloody amateurs!"

"Just remember who let them get away in the first place." Said Bobby.

"Don't fucking start with me. I was drugged. They were gone when I woke up." Said Michael.

"Just don't be having a go at them, when you were meant to be keeping an eye on her."

"She was locked away just fine."

"Then have a word with your damn brother. This is his doing."

They ran round to the back of the building, to where Dennis made his escape. They saw a makeshift platform underneath one of the windows. They climbed up and in through the window, to see two of their guys on the floor. One of them was out cold. And the other was on his hands and knees, holding the back of his head.

"What the fuck happened to you two?" asked Michael.

"They got the jump on us."

"Where's Johnny and Junior?"

"Didn't see them. As soon as we came through that window, we were jumped."

"Right, spread out and find them." Said Michael.

All the men spread out and searched the building. Eventually there was a shout from the third floor.

"FOUND THEM."

Everyone else converged on the apartment where the shouting had come from. When Michael and Bobby walked into the apartment, they saw one of the men trying to untie Johnny and Bobby jnr.

"Let me fucking guess, they got the jump on you too?" said Michael.

"We came into the building nice and quiet, ready to sneak up on them. Once we got inside, we were ambushed at gunpoint. The two guys who killed Garrod, were here. They came out of their hiding places and stopped us. Dennis put a Fucking knife to junior's throat. That brother of yours is fucking crazy."

"Who are the two guys who killed Garrod? Do we know anything about them?"

"They seem to be well connected. Before they left, I heard them telling Dennis, they could protect him and the girl."

"We need to find them. We have the license number from their vehicle, so we need to find out what we can about those two. We have guys trying to catch them as we speak. You two better pray we find them, or you will both be fucked."

"Leave it out Michael." Said Bobby snr.

"The fuck I will Bobby. They fucked up. They will pay if those fuckers get away."

35

"Everyone ok?" I asked, as we finally got away from Brooklyn and through Manhattan. Everyone responded with yesses, so that was a relief.

We finally got through the Lincoln tunnel and across Union city. All we could do right now, was head West and find somewhere to lay up overnight. Then by morning hopefully we would have a location for the heli pick up. The further west we made it, the less distance the helicopter had to cover.

After another hour or so, Danny thought we were being followed.

"You sure it's the same one?"

"Yeah. Black SUV. I noticed it as we came out of Union city, I wanted to be sure before I said anything but its definitely the same one." Said Danny.

"Fucking Deja-vu" I said.

"How's that?"

"Being chased across country. This is what happened with that bloody brief case problem."

"Oh yes." Danny said, laughing. "You do attract the wrong kind of attention."

"I do don't I." I started to chuckle at that point.

"What's so funny?" asked Dennis.

"Just reminiscing on good old times." I said.

"You going to try and lose them? Or are we going to deal with them?" asked Danny.

"I've learnt my lesson. Trying to lose someone doesn't work well. This time we deal with them."

We were on highway Eighty. Just past a small town called Totowa, we pulled off the highway into an industrial area near North Cove Park. Across the way was a development site for housing. It looked like the construction had only recently started, as the area was mostly empty and open land. I pulled into a spot just outside the perimeter fencing and switched off the engine. It wasn't long before was saw headlights coming our way.

It wasn't completely dark out, but it was getting there. The vehicle stopped before it got to us. We couldn't make out what vehicle it was. We couldn't just kick off assuming it was the following SUV. It may have been police checking on the area. We had to wait for whoever it was to make the first move.

"How many weapons do we have?" I asked. Not really aiming the question at anyone in particular.

"I have one of the guns we took from the two guys who came through the window." Said Danny.

"Me too," said Dennis.

"Three guns between us. We should be ok with that." I said. "I'm going to spin this car round so we can get the lights on whoever that is. If it's the SUV follower, we deal with them quickly."

I floored the accelerator and spun the car round to face the other vehicle. Once I was facing them, I put on the main beam and shed some light on the situation. There were three guys slowly making their way towards us. They stopped when the lights illuminated them. We could clearly see that all three of them were carrying weapons. Me and Danny both opened our windows.

"On three" I said.

Once I got to three, what I thought would happen, didn't. On three, Dennis jumped out of the car and started shooting.

"No" I shouted, but it was too late. he shot wildly, not aiming. A couple of seconds was all it was before he was down. I didn't see where he was shot, but he was swearing a lot so I knew he would be ok for a few minutes at least.

Danny got off a couple of shots through his open window, then he jumped out too.

I ended up out of the car too, shooting in the general direction as the armed guys from the SUV. Once I got behind our vehicle, I started aiming my shots. We only had pistols with no extra ammo, so we couldn't afford to waste them. By the time I'd shot one of them Danny already had one down and one running back to his vehicle. We shot out his tyres, he knew his wasn't going anywhere. He started shooting wildly from behind his door, until Danny shot his foot. He went down screaming and dropped his weapon. Danny and I ran towards him and I stopped Danny with a wave of my hand so he wouldn't shoot him.

"We can use him to leave a message." I said.

"Good idea."

He sat there swearing at us. Threatening us with pay back.

"Tell your boss to back off. If he comes near the girl again, he will be next."

I hit him with my pistol and he was out cold.

"We need to get somewhere and get some rest."

"I think we should rest on the move. I'll drive for a few hours, then we swap." Said Danny.

"Ok we'll go with that. First let's see how Dennis is doing.

He was sat against the car holding his arm. Sally had stopped the bleeding using his belt. She was just trying to clean him up a bit.

"How you doing?" I asked.

"I'll live. Just hurts like hell."

"Yeah, getting shot tends to do that."

"We are going to keep moving, no stop overs. You going to be ok with that?"

"Yeah, I'll be fine." Said Dennis.

"Good. Let's get moving."

36

Michael was not happy. One of his men had called him and told him that Dennis and his mates had pulled over near an industrial estate. They were going to get Sally and Dennis and kill the two men who were with them, then call him back for further instructions.

He'd been waiting for nearly three quarters of an hour now. He wasn't a patient man at the best of times, now he just wanted to know that his brother and the girl were back in his care.

He tried calling his guys again. No answer.

"For fuck sake. What the hell is going on? They should have the situation under control bye now."

"All we can do right now, is keep heading towards that industrial area and wait for him to call." Said Bobby.

"We've been waiting long enough. They should have Dennis and the girl now."

That's when his phone started ringing.

"You better have some good news for me."

"They've gone boss. I'm the only one left. The other two are dead. Dennis got away."

"For fuck sake. All you had to do, was get those two back and take out their new friends. Should have done it myself."

"One of them told me to give you a message. You are to leave the girl alone, or you will be next. The police are nearly here, I can see their lights."

"You keep your mouth shut. You hear me? Keep your mouth shut."

"No point going to the industrial area now. We need to keep heading west and try to catch these bastards."

"Stay on highway eighty. Keep heading west" Bobby said into the radio to the vehicle behind.

37

Danny had been driving for three hours, since leaving the industrial area.

"We need to pull over soon. Get some food and something to drink." I said.

"Top up the fuel too." Said Danny.

We found a service station off highway eighty, near a little place called Lamar. We topped up the fuel in the car, got something to eat and drink, then set off again. I took over the driving so Danny could get some shut eye. I decided to call Billy and see where we needed to meet this helicopter.

"Hi Mike."

"We are still heading in your direction. I need to know where we are heading, where do we need to be for this pick up?"

"I'm receiving that information as we speak. Looks like you need to make your way to Manti Ephraim Airport. You go through a town called Salina off highway seventy and head north. The helo will refuel there and bring you back here."

"Will we have any problems getting on the airfield?"

"No. You will be escorted to the helo and your car will be taken care of."

"You've thought of everything as usual."

"That's what I do Mike."

"And you do it well Billy. See you soon."

I ended the call. We had about another 5 hours or so to the airfield in Salina.

All I could think about was getting Sally back to her girls and how best to keep them safe. Sally would want to get back to her life again at some point. Her apartment, her job. The only place for them to be for the time being was Stan's place. That's the safest place for them. I can only assume the beauty salon where she works, will have some kind of memorial thing for Casey. Such a young life taken for no reason. It makes my blood boil when I think about it. They were just walking to work, minding their own business when they were taken off the street just like that. I'd love to make the men responsible for it, pay. I was still planning on grilling Dennis about it, but I'm not sure exactly how much of a part he took in the kidnapping. Sally will no doubt fill me in on that. I guess by what Sally has already told me, that he was trying to help her from the start. The thought had crossed my mind that the message we left for Dennis's brother may end it. But I knew deep down that we, would have to end it. Dennis didn't seem to think his brother would give up, so we would have to stop him and find this Reg guy. He was the ring leader in all of this, so ultimately, he needed to be taken care of, if Sally and her girls were going to be able to carry on as normal.

38

Finally, we made it to the airfield at Selina. As soon as I pulled up to the security gates, our escort was there waiting to take us to the heli.

The other three were all awake now, all sat upright in their seats, waiting to get on the helicopter and get home. Sally especially couldn't wait to see her girls.

"Make sure you all have everything. You leave anything in the car, it will be destroyed. Leave the weapons on the floor, they will be taken care of."

We followed the escort to the heli. We pulled up and got out of the car, as a guy from the escort vehicle came over and got in. He drove away with the escort vehicle following.

We all climbed up into the heli, then Sally got to work with a first aid kit, cleaning Dennis's arm.

"When we get back home, you need to move back in my place for the time being." I said. Looking at Sally.

"You'll get no argument from me on that one. I just need to see my girls."

"I bet they are going to be happy to see you too." Said Danny.

I was glad she didn't argue about moving back in with me. My place was in the confines of Stan's property, so they would be safe there until we were sure they weren't going to get more shit from this, Michael fella.

We were all told to buckle up and get ready to leave. Finally, we could all relax knowing we were heading home.

I had a feeling; this Michael character was going to appear back home at some point. He clearly wasn't the type to give up. We would have to keep our eyes peeled and watch out for him. If he got hold of Sally again, it wouldn't bare thinking about.

39

Eventually we made it home. All tired from lack of sleep We all managed to get a bit of shut eye, but helicopters weren't the most comfortable thing to sleep in. As soon as we climbed down from the helicopter, Sally was running to find the girls. It was still early morning, but the sky was light. Daylight was fast approaching and I was ready for some breakfast. We took Dennis to the medical bay to get his arm looked at, then Danny and myself went to eat. Sally would do her own thing once she'd spent some time with the girls.

"Do you think that will be the end of it?" asked Danny.

"You know as well as I do mate, it's not over."

"We need to keep an eye on Sally and the twins. Maybe keep an eye on her apartment too. Just in case."

"Yes mate. That Michael fella may well turn up again."

Billy walked in all smiles. "Good morning gents. Glad to see you in one piece."

"Morning Billy. How are you doing?"

"Pretty good actually. While you've been out gallivanting, I've had a couple of guys keep an eye on that address where Reg is supposed to live, in San Diego. We've confirmed that he does live there. He is in and out of there all the time. We are keeping the guys over there watching him, so we know where he is when you guys want to visit him."

"Again, you've thought of everything. We will be wanting to speak to him soon. How's Stan and Carol doing?"

"Like a couple of love birds. Always together. You couldn't part them with a pry bar."

That made me laugh. It was hard to imagine Stan, all loved up, but why not. Everyone deserves a bit of happiness.

"I'm going to take my coffee back down to my place. Stop bye later and I'll show you what I have."

"Will do mate. Thanks again for all your help."

"Stop thanking me. It's what I do." Shouted Billy over his shoulder as he walked out of the room.

"This Reg character is the main man isn't he? If we speak to him, we may be able to straighten this out."

"We can try mate, but I'm not so sure it will be that simple. He had Sally kidnapped because of something John did a few years ago. He won't forget about it just because we ask him to."

"Yeah, good point. We may have to be quite persuasive."

"That we can do."

We finished our breakfast and went to freshen up. After I'd showered and got fresh clothes on, I went to check on Sally and the girls. They were still in their room in Stan's main building. I knocked and walked in and both the girls ran over and hugged me. I could see that they had been crying, Sally too. I was just happy that they were reunited. I would make sure that they were never separated from each other like that, ever again.

It was now time to go and see Billy, see what he has for me.

"Ah Mike. You all fed and watered now?"

"Yes mate, couldn't eat anything else right now. What do you have for me Billy?"

"Well like I said. We've confirmed the house in San Diego belongs to that Reg character. We have men watching him. When you are ready to go and see him, we'll know exactly where he is."

"Ok good. Anything new?"

"Yes. I was hoping to have more, by the time you got down here, but this is proving difficult.

"I received a message about an hour or so before I saw you in the canteen. When I say I received it, it's actually for you."

"From who?"

"Don't know yet."

"What does it say?"

"Don't know that either."

"What do you know?"

"I have a message on my computer addressed to you. Only trouble is, it's encrypted or password protected. I can't find a way to open it right now. Someone has gone to great lengths to make sure only you see it."

"It must be from someone who knows I work with you guys. But why make it hard to get into. If you can't open it, I sure as hell won't be able to."

"Whoever sent it obviously thinks you will figure it out. "It could be a simple thing. Something maybe only you and this person knows."

"That doesn't narrow it down much. If you have any clues, let me know. I have something I need to do. Will check in with you later."

"Ok. I will keep working on it."

40

LATE THE PREVIOUS EVENING

Michael was still seething with the fact his men had lost Sally and Dennis.

"We need to catch them before they get to wherever it is they are going."

"We've probably lost them already. All we need to do is head towards her apartment and wait for her to show up. She's bound to go there at some point."

"Why are you so fucking chilled out about all this. The boss isn't going to be best pleased about losing her."

"No point getting wound up over something you can't change."

"You're getting soft Bobby. That's why those boys of yours aren't up to the job."

"You keep having a go about my boys, me and you are going to fall out."

"Then get them in line. They need to be on the ball when we get back there."

Bobby just sat there shaking his head.

"Boss" A voice called over the radio.

"Go ahead" said Bobby.

"Just heard from a friend at Salina Airport, Kansas. He has seen Sally and Dennis in a vehicle with two other men. Seems they are heading towards a part of the airfield where there is a helicopter waiting."

"Shit. Tell him, he needs to stop them. He needs to do whatever it takes."

"Will tell him boss."

"How far out are we?" asked Michael.

"About Forty minutes boss." Said the driver.

"Shit. If they are nearly at the helicopter, we won't make it. Get us there fast."

"Going as fast as I can boss."

41

I went and found Danny. I wanted to go and check out
Sally's apartment. After finding him, we set off over
there.

"You got a list of the things she needs?" said Danny.

"She told me what she needed. Clothes mainly. I just
want to check the place. I have a feeling that we will be
seeing Dennis's brother again. Just want to make sure
they haven't been back there. See if we can spot anyone
hanging around."

"No harm in checking. You think they will come back
this way?"

"They seemed hell bent on getting Sally and Dennis
back. I think it's a safe bet that they'll be back."

We parked up near Sally's apartment. Walked round the
block and got to her place. All seemed ok so far. No
damaged door. I used her key to unlock the door, then
we walked in. Things were different inside; the place had
been trashed.

"Shit. Someone really gave this place a going over."

"There's no way they could get back here that quick."

"Maybe they had someone else do it."

"Only explanation. But why trash the place? What were
they looking for? If they only wanted her, why do this?"

"To send a message." Said Danny.

"Yeah, guess so."

"I'll grab some of her clothes and we'll head back."

After getting what Sally needed, we locked up, got back to our car and headed back home.

"She wont be happy about that." Said Danny.

"Let's just keep it to ourselves for now. No point worrying her any more than she may already be."

"Good idea."

We got back to Stan's place and gave Sally her things. After making sure her and the girls were ok, we went to see Billy.

"So, what's the plan now?"

"I think it's time we paid a little visit to that Reg character. Billy can tell us exactly where he is."

"We need to stop this. If we convince him to call his dogs off. Sally and the girls can get back to their lives."

"You think it will be that easy?"

"Probably not. That's why we will go via the armoury. At least we will be prepared."

"Good call."

Billy was pleased to see us as usual.

He turned to speak to us, then looked straight back at his computer again. "Hello gents" he said. "Looks like good timing" he said, as his computer pinged.

"Looks like we may be closer to opening that message."

He tapped a few keys on his keyboard. "It needs a six-digit passcode to open it. My guess is that it's something you would obviously know Mike. Any idea?"

"It could be absolutely anything."

"True, but it's unique to you I'm sure of it. This message was sent for you. Whoever sent it only wants you to see it, so is there any six-digit reference you can think of? Or six letter word that may be unique between you and another person?"

"No idea."

"Could this be to do with your military days? Army numbers? Nicknames?"

"My army number had six digits but I doubt it would be that."

"Can't hurt to try. What is it?"

I told him my old army number and the results shocked even Billy.

"Wow. It was as easy as that." Billy said with amusement.

"You shitting me?" I said.

"Nope. It's ready to open. You want to look yourself?"

"No mate. Just open it."

"Ok."

Billy went into another screen and put in the six-digit number.

He turned the screen a little so that all three of us could see it and pressed the enter key.

IM NOT DEAD

"What the fuck is this?" said Danny.

"Fucked if I know mate. can you see who it's from?"

"No. The computer is still trying to figure that out."

"Can you send a message back?"

"Doesn't look like it. If I figure out a way to reply, I'll let you know."

"Thanks mate. we need to know where Reg is. Is he home?"

"Let me see." He typed a message on his keyboard and a couple of seconds later he received a reply.

"Our guys say he is still home."

"Good. We are going to head over there."

"Do me a favour. Take a couple of guys with you. That place has a lot of security."

"Ok. Can you have a couple of guys meet us at the armoury"

"Will do. Keep me up to date what's going on."

"You let me know as soon as you have more on where that message came from."

42

After leaving the armoury with our choice of weapons, we set off for San Diego.

It took us nearly Three hours to get over there, traffic wasn't great. We were looking for Cypress Avenue, apparently the house we were looking for had the only u-shaped driveway in the street so it shouldn't be that hard to find. It was pretty much in the corner of the estate, on a bend in the road. That would be handy if the shit hit the fan. I always like to look for potential escape routes when I go somewhere I haven't been before. Old habits die hard. It was around Five PM when we parked the car. We left it about a hundred yards from Reg's place, away from other driveways so it didn't attract attention.

The Two guys who were with us walked the opposite way from us, and waited out of the way until we radioed them. This time of year, sun down wasn't until around Eight PM. We didn't want to wait until then so Danny and myself walked straight to the house. No point in putting it off. We arrived outside the driveway where Two Suv's and an old mustang sat in the evening sun.

"How do you want to play this?" said Danny.

"No point messing around. We tell them why we are here, and just go with it."

"Sounds good to me."

We walked up the driveway to the house, and were stopped before we got to the door.

"This is private property. You need to leave." Said a guy, wearing a dark suit and dark shades.

"We are here to see Reg." I said.

"Who are you?"

"We are friends of Sally Stibbings." I said.

"There is no one here by that name. You need to leave. Now."

"We aren't leaving until we've spoken to Reg."

"Everything alright Frank?" said another suited up guy as he walked over to where we were.

"These two are refusing to leave until they've spoken to Reg."

"What do you want with Reg?"

"As we told your friend here, we are friends of Sally Stibbings. And we want to speak to Reg."

The guy didn't hide the shock on his face. He clearly knew about the Sally situation.

"Wait here." He said. "Keep them here" he said to his mate.

We stood on the driveway in awkward silence for about Five minutes, then the guy in the suit came back out.

"Follow me" he said.

We followed him to the house, but instead of going in, he took us down a foot path around the side of the house. We walked round to the back of the house where there was a big swimming pool with a handful of bikini clad girls lying around and splashing in the pool. There were Three or Four guys hanging around a small bar on the patio area. When we walked into the area, everyone turned their heads and stared at us. I couldn't tell if they knew why we were here or not, but if this turned bad, we would have a few guys to deal with. We followed the security guy to the far end of the rear yard where a guy wearing a cream linen suit was sat at a small table with a couple of suited guys standing near bye.

"Sit down gentlemen" he said as we walked over to him. We took a seat opposite him.

"As you can see, I have a few friends round and I'd like to get back to them so let's make this quick."

"You know why we are here. You need to call your boys off, then we can all move on."

"If that's what you came all this way for, you are wasting your time."

"The guy who upset your robbery plans all those years ago, is dead. He's gone, move on." I said.

"I'm afraid it's not that simple, you see, he robbed me of the life I should be living right now."

"We've come here to sort this out. You won't get anything from Sally, so tell your guys to leave her alone."

Reg laughed at this.

"I think you underestimate the situation. See, by the time my guys finish with her, she will give up everything she owns."

Me and Danny looked at each other. This guy clearly had no idea that Sally was no longer being held captive.

I put my hand up to scratch my ear, and discreetly clicked the ear piece on my radio mic and alerted our other two guys to stand bye. I'd never tried these new ear pieces before, so I hoped they worked. I had a decision to make, and quick. Do I tell him that Sally is no longer being held? Or do I just keep him thinking that she is? I decided to tell him how it is.

"I guess you need to be brought up to speed. Sally is no longer being held by your guys. We have her back, and that's the way its staying. Keep your guys away from her."

I nodded at Danny, and we both stood up to leave.

"Where the fuck do you think you're going? What do you mean, she isn't being held? That's impossible."

"Like I said. We have her back. I'm guessing your guys don't keep you in the loop."

I put my hand up and tapped my ear piece again. I had a feeling; things were about to go bad.

43

Our Two men sneaked up to the guy dressed in a suit and wearing dark glasses. Before the suited guy could find out what was going on, he was out cold. One of the guys got him in a throat lock and put him to sleep.

They laid him to the side of the driveway and moved on to find the other security guy.

He spotted them before they saw him. He pulled out a gun and aimed at them. "Put down your weapons and stay where you are."

The two guys turned towards him with their weapons raised. "I suggest you put your weapon down. I won't ask you again."

The security guy realised he was out gunned and slowly bent down to put his gun on the floor, but changed his mind. As he started to raise his weapon again, the two guys took him down. Both shooting him in his centre mass. He was dead before he hit the floor.

They moved on to the front door.

"What was that?" said Reg.

He pulled out his own weapon pointing it at Danny and myself. The two guys standing behind him followed suit. His guests were all starting to look a little nervous now. Two of the men by the bar pulled out their own weapons. At this point the girls all ran towards the house.

We didn't know at this point, what was going to happen next. We couldn't pull out our weapons right now. We would be dead before we got our hands on them. I tried to manoeuvre myself so that Reg would have his back to the house when he was looking in our direction.

"If this is something to do with you, I suggest you tell whoever you brought with you, to show themselves."

"It's just the two of us. We didn't bring anyone else." Said Danny.

At this point the girls who ran into the house started to scream.

Reg put his weapon up to my head. "You better fucking tell whoever is in there, to come out with their hands up."

"We didn't bring anyone else" I was sure I was pushing my luck, but we needed a way out of this, and giving up our guys wasn't it.

Then the shit hit the fan. The two guys at the bar holding weapons, were the first to get it. The shots came from inside the house. The two men were put down quick. The other guys at the bar area ran.

Our two guys then appeared through the patio doors.

Reg was quick to get himself behind me, still holding his weapon to my head.

"You better drop those mother fucking guns right now" he shouted at our guys.

The two of them remained where they were, weapons still aimed at Reg and his men.

One of our guys told Reg's men to drop their weapons.

"Fuck you" was the only answer they got.

One of the guy's kept his weapon aimed towards Reg.
Our other guy took out the two guys near Reg.
He took a bullet to his shoulder before they went down.
He seemed to take it well, and pointed his weapon back
in Reg's direction.

Stan's guys were well trained and disciplined. I couldn't
fault the way they operated. I was just glad they were on
our side.

Our guys spread out. I could see they were trying to get a
better angle on Reg. He was keeping as much of himself
behind me as possible. If I were in his shoes, I would
have done the same.

"Put the fucking weapons down now." Said Reg.

"Look, we can sort this out. Let's just relax and talk
about this." I said.

I should have kept my mouth shut. I felt Reg move
slightly and then felt a sharp pain in my head. I noticed
Danny dive towards me, And I heard gun shots. Then my
world went dark.

44

Michael had been informed that Sally and her friends got away. The inside man at the airfield wasn't quick enough to stop them. As usual Michael was not happy about it. "Let's just get over to her fucking apartment and find them. I want everyone spread out when we get over there. We will keep eyes on the apartment. The rest of you will keep searching the area until we find them. Is that understood?"

All of his guys answered on the radio's.

"You make sure your boys don't fuck up again."

"Now you listen to me. This was all your fuck up in the first place. They got unlucky back there. They wont let that happen again. So shut your fucking mouth and get on with your part of the job." Said Bobby.

"I will do my part. Just make sure they do theirs." Said Michael.

"We will be there in the early hours. We get there, spread out and be ready to grab them."

"Make sure a couple of our vehicles are ready to move at any time. We may need them to follow them if found."

"Everyone knows what they are doing. Just fucking relax."

"I'll relax when we have that Bitch back. Not before."

"You called the boss yet?"

"No. He doesn't need to know just yet. We will have her back soon and he will never know."

"You'd better prey he doesn't."

45

My head hurt like hell, and for some reason, so did my right shoulder.

"Nice of you to join us again."

I turned my head to see Stan and Danny standing near the bed.

"What the fuck happened?" I said.

"You were hit over the head and shot." Said Danny.

"Shot by who?"

"We think it was Reg. He hit you and as you went down our guys took him out, but we think he got a shot off as he went down. Luckily only to your shoulder. It went in and out through flesh, no bone or muscle damage. Apart from the pain you have now, it will cause you no more problems once it's healed."

"That's good to know. That bastard could have killed me."

"Well he didn't. Let's be thankful for that." Said Stan.

"Sally and the girls ok?"

"They are fine. Dennis is healing nicely too. We have given him a room to stay in until this is all dealt with."

"Good. I will pop and see them soon. Billy found out anymore about that message?"

"Nothing major. He said he will go through it when he see's you next."

"That's a weird one. Why not just message me personally?"

"Billy will be able to answer that too." Said Stan.

"Sally has mentioned that she wants to give up her apartment and stay here. We will have to organise moving her stuff out." Said Danny.

"I'm glad about that. They will be better off here. At least for the time being. I need to go and see Billy."

"No you don't. You stay right where you are. I'll get Billy to come to you." Said Stan.

"Thanks. I need to know who sent that message."

"I'll get him straight over here."

Stan walked out of the room mid call to Billy.

"We need to plan our next move, regarding Dennis's brother." I said.

"I think we should wait for him to come to us. We know he wont give up on getting Sally and his brother back, so let him do the leg work."

"I agree. We should just be ready. We don't know where or when he will appear. It will most likely be soon. We need to make sure Sally and the girls are protected Twenty Four Seven."

"That we can do. I'm going for Coffee. You want anything?"

"Coffee and something to eat mate, thanks."

"Be back soon."

A few minutes after Danny left, Billy turned up.

"How's the patient doing?" he said.

"Not bad thanks mate."

"Can I get you anything?"

"Danny is sorting that thanks. What have you got for me?"

"I managed to communicate with whoever sent that message. I mean communicate as far as getting a reply." Billy opened up his laptop and showed me what he had.

"As you can see, I tried to find out who it is but got nowhere. All I got was this reply.

I WANT TO MEET WITH MIKE.

"Nothing since."

"Why did this message come through to you in the first place?"

"When you first came to us, we gave you a mobile phone. That mobile and all mobile phones belonging to any one of you guys working or staying here, are watched by my computer. If anything flags up as out of the ordinary, the computer will intercept that message and send it to me. I know you guys do a lot out of the ordinary, but this was flagged because of the mention of death. I then have to check the contents and decide how to act on it, if at all. In this case I needed your help to open it."

"Ok. Makes sense."

"Do you have any idea yet, who it could be."

"Not a clue mate. Wish I did."

"If I come up with anything else I'll let you know. What do you want to do about meeting this person?"

"Once I'm back on my feet, I'll decide then."

"Ok. Let me know and I'll organise it. Better get back. Feel better soon Mike."

"Thanks mate."

Danny returned with Coffee and pie and chips. They know how to look after people here. Probably why I love being here.

46

After eating, I took more pain killers for my shoulder,
then went to see Sally. Her and the girls were back in my
place. It was early afternoon and I walked a little
unsteadily across the yard to my place. My head was
banging but the sun was shining, it was a beautiful day.
I don't know what drugs they gave me in the medical
bay, but I slept like a baby all night.
I got over to my place and the girls ran over and hugged
me. They'd been doing homework, so they were glad to
get away from it for a minute.
"Come on girls. Finish your homework then you can do
what you want."
"Ok Mum." They both said in unison.
They went off to finish what they were doing and Sally
made me coffee.
"How are you feeling?" she asked as she handed me my
drink and sat down.
"A bit sore, but I'll live."
"You and the twins doing, ok?"

"The girls are fine. They haven't really asked me much about what happened. They are just glad to have me back."

"I bet they are. They look happy, so that's good. Stan tells me you want to stay here for a while."

"I don't feel comfortable staying at the apartment now. We are safer here."

"We will arrange getting your stuff over here."

"I've been meaning to ask you about Stan. What is it he does exactly? He has this big place here. Some people live here, people just keep coming and going at all hours. Just seems a bit odd."

"It is a busy place I know. The guys here are often called vigilantes. Stan set this place up years ago after spending a few years doing the work of the police. The guys here basically just do the jobs that police aren't interested in. Some people need help dealing with issues that the police take forever to deal with, or just blow off altogether. One of the biggest jobs they've dealt with is the one John was helping with. The one I came over here to deal with."

"It's kinda nice knowing there are people out there who like to see justice done and want to help people. Does he get paid for the things he does? Do you? After all you live here now too."

"Stan is a wealthy man. Most of what he does, he funds himself. Some things are paid for by clients if needed, but he mainly deals with all that. Myself and the guys who work for him, get paid well for what we do. Most of the jobs we take on aren't related to violence. But some turn out like that."

"So that's why the police don't get involved?"

"Pretty much. Unless Stan contacts them for any reason, they tend to leave us alone."

"John would have loved all this action."

"I know. He would have been a valuable member here."

"I do miss him. The girls don't ask about him all the time now, so they are obviously getting used to the fact he has gone."

"We have his memorial near by, so they can visit him whenever they want."

"Do you think Dennis's brother will turn up again?"

"We expect him too. But don't worry about it, you and the girls are safe here. You will all have a security detail with you every time you leave this place. He won't get near you or the girls."

"What will happen if he turns up?"

"We will deal with him."

"I need to get to the apartment soon and sort things out."

"No need to worry about that. We will have everything moved out and brought over here. You can then sort out what you need to."

"I'm not used to everything being organised for me. I could get used to this." She said with a chuckle.

I was glad she was happy about it. I didn't want her knowing that her apartment had been trashed.

"I would like to go back to the salon and see the ladies there. Not sure they know about Casey and I'd like to have a catch up with them."

"I'll get that arranged for you. When would you like to go?"

"Some time the next couple of days would be good."

"I'll get that sorted for you."

"Thanks. We appreciate everything you are doing for us Mike."

"No need to thank me. As long as you and the girls are safe and happy, that's good enough for me. I must go and see Billy now. Got some things to sort out."

We both stood up and she threw her arms around me and hugged me. I then turned and walked out the door.

I still had feelings for her, but that was something I planned on keeping to myself from now on.

47

Billy was glued to his computer screens as usual. he signalled me to give him a couple of minutes. He was obviously in the middle of something important.

"Sorry about that Mike. You should have called. I would have come to you."

"My legs still work fine mate. I cant be lying in bed all day. Not my style."

"What can I do for you?"

"First thing, can we organise a security detail to take Sally to her old work place? In the next day or so?"

"No problem. I will sort that out for her."

"I would like to meet this person who sent that message. I can't stop thinking about it, and it's bugging me who the fuck it is."

"Will send a message now. When do you want to meet?"

"Anytime soon." I said.

Billy started tapping keys. I don't know how many words he could type per minute, but he was fast.

"I've messaged and said that you want to meet. Need to wait for a reply now."

We didn't have to wait long. The message came back quickly. We looked at the screen.

WHEN AND WHERE?

"Tell them tomorrow. After lunch. Culver City Park. Near the car park. One PM."

The reply came straight back.

I'LL BE THERE. JUST MIKE.

"This will be interesting. Wish I knew who it could be."

"I will arrange for you to be followed. Can't let you go alone."

"Tell them to keep out of sight."

"Will do. I'll arrange for Sally to be escorted to the salon tomorrow lunch time. Around Twelve ish."

"Excellent mate. Thanks. I'll let her know."

48

I left Billy's and went to let Sally know that she would be picked up the following lunch time.

There was nothing I needed to do for the rest of the day, so I just chilled out. Sally and the girls were happy. All was quiet.

I had no idea who this mystery person was who wanted to meet me. I'd been racking my brains, trying to figure out who it could be. I would make sure I had a weapon with me. You never know.

The rest of the day passed quietly. Catching up with Stan and Carol. Having a couple of beers with Danny, and a couple of the lads. It made a change not having to rush around here there and everywhere.

After a good night's sleep, I showered and went for breakfast. Once I washed that down with a couple of coffee's and chatted shit with some of the lads, I went to check on Sally.

"You ready to go?"

"Just about"

"Your security detail will be here in a little while. They will be keeping an eye on you. They will wait outside the Salon whilst you are visiting."

"You think we will have a problem?" she said.

"It's just a precaution."

"There is no telling what my brother may do. That's why I'm going with her." Said Dennis

"How's the arm?"

"It'll be fine"

"Any problems, you head straight back here."

"We will," said Sally.

"I'll leave you to it. Let me know when you are back. I will be out myself for a little while. I'll pop and see you when I get back."

After leaving Sally and Dennis, I went to the armoury to get my weapon, then went to meet up with the guys who were going to be tailing me for this meeting. I decided to leave a few minutes earlier than planned, and walk there instead. Stan's place was on Baldwin hill. The Park we were meeting in was at the foot of Baldwin hill. I could drive there, but what would be the point of that. It was a beautiful day, may as well enjoy the sunshine.

It was Twelve Thirty now, Sally would be at the Salon having a catch up with her old work colleagues.

I went to see Billy, to make sure nothing had changed, then left for the park. It wouldn't take me long to get there. My plan was to get there early and find a spot to watch the carpark. That way I could see who turned up. Once I got to the park, I had to make my way down, through to the carpark. People were enjoying the sunshine. Some guys were throwing a Frisbee around. Some were kicking a football about. One of the Baseball fields had a big group of people practicing. There was a

139

small carpark next to this Baseball field, so I hoped the person I was meeting realised I meant the main carpark. That's the one I was heading for. I was looking for a spot with a clear view of the carpark when my phone buzzed in my pocket. It was Billy. Knowing my luck, this person had decided they didn't want to meet after all.

"Billy, what's up?"

"You need to get back here Mike. We just received a call from the security detail watching Sally. They said they were concerned about a couple of vehicles parked nearby. Three black SUV's all parked near the Salon. At least two up in each vehicle, that's just the ones they can see."

"Shit. Ok I'm on my way. Get Danny and the guys ready. I'll be there as soon as I can."

"They are all ready. Head back up via the main road. They will pick you up on route."

"Will do. Keep me up to date Billy."

I ended the call and started running towards the main road, followed by the two guys who were tailing me. I would head back up until I met up with Danny.

The meeting would have to wait.

49

Michael was sitting in the back of an SUV, giving out orders as usual. There were Three of them parked near the Salon where Sally worked. All spread out, watching. Two more vehicles full of guys were watching Sally's apartment.

"Heads up. We have a vehicle pulling up outside the Salon. A dark blue Chrysler."

All of the guys in all of the vehicles watched as the vehicle pulled up and Sally and Dennis stepped out and walked into the Salon.

"This is too easy." Michael laughed. "Where are all of their new friends?"

"I guess they under estimate us." Said Bobby.

"Their mistake. We wait for them to come out, then follow them."

It wasn't long before the men in the blue sedan spotted the SUV's. One of them called in to report their concerns.

"I'm going to go and have a closer look. If anything happens, get those two out here and get them back home." Said the other guy.

"Be careful mate." Said his Buddy.

The guy climbed out of the car, checked his weapon under his jacket, and casually walked towards one of the SUV's.

"Boss, you seeing this?"

"Yes, let him near, see what he wants. Be ready."

"You want me to take him out?"

"Only if you have to."

The man continued to walk towards them. He walked up to the SUV as the driver put down the window.

"Can I help you?" said the driver.

"Yes. I noticed you and all of your mates are watching us. What do you want?"

"We aren't watching anybody. We are just sitting here having a break from our journey."

"This is a bit of an odd place to sit for a break."

"Fuck off mate. Leave us alone if you know what's good for you."

The guy took a step back from the SUV.

"No need to be like that. Just have your break somewhere else."

"You got something to hide?" said the driver.

"Just move on and leave us to our business."

"We will move on when we are good and ready."

The guy turned to walk away and spoke into his mic.

"Get them out here, we need to leave."

The other one of Sally's security guys got out of his car and rushed inside the Salon.

"Boss, looks like they are on the move. What shall we do?"

"Change of plan, take that guy out. Don't let them get away." Said Michael.

The driver from the SUV pulled out his silenced weapon and shot the security guy in the back as he was walking away.

The other security guy rushed out of the Salon followed closely by Sally and Dennis. He noticed his buddy was lying in a pool of blood and the SUVs were closing in on the Salon.

"Get her in that car and get back home, NOW." He shouted as he threw his keys to Dennis.

He started to lay down fire on the SUVs, trying to keep them back.

Sally and Dennis got into the car and sped off.

"Johnny, Junior, get after them. Bring them back to me alive." Said Michael over the radio.

"On it." Said Johnny.

They turned their SUV around and sped off after them. The other SUVs stopped and the guys got out and started firing their weapons towards the lone security guy. He was hunched down behind another vehicle.

Michael soon realised that no one was coming to help this security guy, so he ordered his driver to get off after Sally and Dennis. He and his men jumped back into his vehicle and set off after Johnny and Junior, leaving the rest of his crew to deal with him.

He managed to get another message to Billy.

"I'm taking fire outside the Salon. I've sent Dennis and Sally back in my car. I'm out numbered. Sean is down.

Not sure how long I can hold them off. Two of their vehicles have raced off after Sally."

"We have a team on their way right now. They will be there soon." Said Billy.

The shooting continued. He took out a couple of Michael's men. He was managing to hold them off for a few minutes, then he took a round to his leg. He kept firing back then ended up out of ammo.

"Shit." He said to himself. His partner was to far away to grab his weapon so he just had to try and get away. He made it round the corner of the block before his world went dark.

50

I was running like hell up to Stan's place. Before I was half way Danny and the guys pulled up. Two vehicles full of guys.

Danny handed me an automatic rifle and a bullet proof vest.

"what's going on mate?" I said.

"Looks like they found Sally. One of the security guys has been taken down. The other was trying to hold them off last I heard."

"What about Sally. Where is she?"

"The security guy told Dennis to get her back here. He gave them his keys."

"Lets keep an eye out for them. We need to get that guy some support."

"That's where we are heading. Stan is standing by for when Sally and Dennis get there."

"They may go back a different way. We may miss them anyway."

"We will be informed when they get back." Said Danny.

"Good. Let's just get our guy back and go home."

My phone went off in my pocket. Billy again.

"What's happening?"

"Security guys are both down. One confirmed, the other we have lost contact with. Sally and Dennis should hopefully be back here soon. It seems that One or Two of their vehicles has given chase to Sally"

"Shit. We will have to find them. We will split up and look for them. Let us know if they turn up."

"Will do."

I radioed our Second vehicle and we split up to follow different routes. we needed to make sure they got back safely.

We were driving around for another Ten to Fifteen minutes when we heard over the radio that our other vehicle has spotted a vehicle down the hillside in flames. There was an SUV at the side of the road, with a couple of guys standing looking down at the burning vehicle.

"Where exactly are you?"

"We are back on Baldwin Hill. We are going to get out and find out what happened."

"We are on our way" I said.

"I fucking hope that isn't sally's vehicle. This is not good. Get us there quick" I yelled at our driver.

"We are taking fire. Four guys shooting at us."

"We will soon be there. Hold them off until we get there."

"We are trying. They have an arsenal with them."

We heard an explosion over the radio.

"Man down. Man down. Two of ours are down. They have god damn RPGs."

This was not going well at all. As we were getting the radio feed, an SUV sped past us in the opposite direction.

"Mike?" the driver shouted.

I looked towards the fleeing SUV.

"Carry on to Baldwin Hill. That must be a different one.
Our guys are still getting heat from the other SUV."
Our driver stamped hard back on the gas. We were
Thirty seconds out now.

"We are coming up to you now." I radioed ahead.
When we pulled up next to our other guys, they were
taking a shit load of gun fire. We all jumped out of our
vehicle and joined in the gun fight. I really wanted to see
what vehicle was burning down the hillside, but the gun
fire was to heavy to try and take a look right now.
Recognising Two of the guys from the SUV, I was
fuelled with rage. I knew at that point it was Sally's car
down the hill. The Two guys were from Dennis's
warehouse apartment back in New York.

I lost my shit at that point.

"Cover me." I shouted.

I ran towards their SUV with no regard for my safety. To
their credit, my guys put down a rain of fire on the guys
at the SUV. When I got there, I launched myself at the
first guy, slamming the butt of my rifle into his face. He
was out before he hit the deck. His mates were more
concerned about me now, than my guys. They all turned
to try and take me down, but my guys followed up with
another massive barrage of fire as they ran towards the
SUV. One of the guys from Dennis's apartment came at
me, so I pulled my knife and let his momentum throw
him onto the blade. He obviously didn't see I was

holding it. By the time I pushed him out of the way, it was pretty much all over. One of our guys was lying face down between our vehicle and the SUV. He'd been shot in the head.

Danny and another of our buddy's had one of them on the floor with a chest wound. He was the other one from the warehouse apartment.

I ran over to look down the hillside. The vehicle was totally engulfed. I could make out what I thought to be, a figure lying a few yards away from the vehicle.

Scrambling down the hillside, I realised it was Dennis. How he got out of that car was a miracle.

I got to him to find he was still breathing. His arms were burnt and so was one side of his face. One of my guys turned up next to me.

"He still alive?"

"Just about" I said.

I could see a burning skeleton in the Passenger seat. I knew it was Sally. This was unbelievable. I was meant to protect her. I promised John I would make sure she was ok.

More guys came down the hillside.

"Let's get him back. He needs medical attention."

Two of the guys carried Dennis back up the hill to our vehicle.

"And finish those motherfuckers off." I shouted pointing up the hill towards the SUV.

I slumped down with my head in my hands. I couldn't believe this was happening. The girls have lost both parents now. How will I explain this?

Hearing a couple of shots, I knew the SUV guys were now finished off.

51

A few minutes earlier.

Michael was trying to catch up with Bobby's boys.
"Put your foot down" he shouted at the driver.
"Where are you" he called over the radio.
"Now heading up Baldwin Hill. Right behind them."
Said Bobby jnr.
"Stop them now. I want them caught. We aren't far
behind."
Just then, Dennis tried to cut them off. As he went to pull
towards them, Bobby's driver swerved, causing Dennis
to over steer and end up back in front of them. As he did
so, Bobby's driver caught the rear quarter of Dennis's
car and put them into a spin. He braked hard and
watched as Dennis skidded over the edge of the
embankment. The car flipped upside down and
continued to roll down the hill, finally stopping against a
tree.
"Shit man. What was that?" Bobby jnr said to his driver.
"I was just trying to avoid being pushed over the edge."
They all got out of the SUV and stared in disbelief. The
car started smoking, closely followed by flames.

It was only a few seconds before Dennis came to again.
Once he realised what was going on, he looked over at

Sally. She wasn't moving. He tried to free her, but couldn't. He untangled himself and stumbled round to Sally's side of the car. He was trying to free her but the flames were getting worse. His arms were starting to burn but he didn't give up. He kept trying to free her until his face was burning and he couldn't take anymore. The heat was just too much. He fell back to the floor as the flames engulfed Sally.

There were no screams, just the sound of the flames consuming her.

Dennis then passed out.

Michael pulled up behind Bobby's SUV. He jumped out and ran over to where they were standing.

"What the fuck did you do." Shouted Michael.

"Sorry boss. They were trying to run us off the road."

"I said I wanted them alive, you idiot."

With that, Michael pulled out his weapon and shot the driver in the head.

"You fuckers are useless" he said to Bobby and Johnny.

"I have a good mind to put a hole in the pair of you too."

"Stop" shouted Bobby snr. "It wasn't their fault."

They heard screeching as a vehicle skidded to a stop. Men jumped out of the vehicle with weapons and Michael and his guys started shooting at them.

"Bobby get in the car, we are out of here."

Michael and Bobby jumped back in their SUV with their driver.

"Get us out of here" Michael shouted to his driver.

"You lot finish this." He shouted out of the window, to Bobby jnr and Johnny.

"No no. They come with us." Shouted Bobby snr.

"We have more important things to worry about now. We have to go and tell the boss what's happened. Whose shoulders do you think this will land on. Mine as fucking usual."

At that point they noticed a car speeding towards them in the opposite direction. As it passed them, they saw who was in the vehicle.

"Shit. That was the guy who helped Dennis. We need to turn back." Said Bobby snr.

"The fuck we are. Your boys can deal with it."

"They will be out numbered."

"The fire power they have in their vehicle will help them deal with them"

"Turn this damn vehicle around, now." Shouted Bobby. Michael pulled out his gun and pointed it at Bobby's head.

"We are not turning back." He said through gritted teeth.

"So, sit back and shut the fuck up."

52

Once we got back to Stan's, we took Dennis straight to the medical bay. There wasn't much they couldn't deal with. They would sort out his burns and make him comfortable while he healed.

We would sort out a memorial for Sally. It would be at the same spot as John's.

That would be better for the girls, to have them together.

I still couldn't think how I was going to tell the girls.

They'd only just got their mother back, now she was gone again. For ever.

I knew one thing for sure. I would find Dennis's brother and make him suffer.

The plan now, was to get a team together and go and find that piece of shit.

I went to round up some guys and go through what we were going to do.

I received a message from Billy, telling me he needed to see me.

I replied, letting him know I would be there soon.

About an hour later, Stan walked in and pulled me to one side.

"Mike. You really need to go and see Billy. I will walk you down."

"What's going on"

"You'll see."

We were soon at Billy's basement.

"What's so important mate?" I said.

"I'm not sure you'd believe me of I told you. That person you were meant to meet earlier today, is now standing outside the front gate."

"Why are they here? Who is it?"

"I think you need to see for yourself." Said Billy.

Stan stood aside as Billy swivelled his screen round towards me. I looked at the screen.

Billy zoomed in on the person standing at the security gate.

"What the fuck. How is this possible." I said to no one in particular.

"Is this a joke?"

"I said you wouldn't believe me." Said Billy. "He turned up at the gate a while ago. He said he wanted to talk to you. The guys told him to get lost, but he is refusing to leave until you've spoken."

"Shall we let him in?"

"No. I'm going out there to see what's going on."

It took me ten minutes to walk over to the front gate.

"Open the gates" I said to the security guys.

The gates opened and I walked through.

"Hello Mike" the person said.

I had no words at that moment. We stood there in silence for a good minute.

"Say something"

The only words I could say at that moment were.

"You better have a damn good reason, for letting people think you were dead."

The final instalment of the Bound trilogy.

The Final Bound, follows Mike and his friends through this fast-paced action-packed finale.

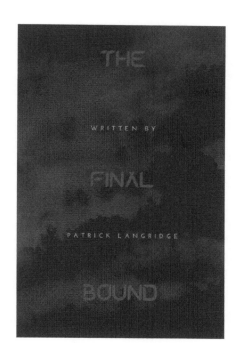

THE

WRITTEN BY

FINAL

PATRICK LANGRIDGE

BOUND

COMING SOON.

Printed in Great Britain
by Amazon

65504561R00097